THE DATING DANCE

By Danielle Nowell

CHAPTER 1

Outside the Apollo Theater, the skies had opened up, and it was raining cats and dogs. Inside the theater, there was a growing standing ovation. Sarah stood up, clapping along with the rest of the theater goers. Meanwhile, up on stage, eight ballerinas took a bow.

"That was a fantastic performance," exclaimed Sarah, who jumped up and down with excitement, feeling lucky to have just witnessed that performance of *Swan Lake*. Sarah's friend Jessie enjoyed the performance herself, although she didn't find herself quite as exhilarated by the performance as her ballet-loving friend. "Yes, it was quite something," mused Jessie.

Sarah and Jessie started toward the exits, donning their rain jackets and preparing their umbrellas. "Man, this weather is something," Sarah said, zipping up her raincoat.

"I don't remember the last time we had a good bit of sunshine. I guess that's living in Grenvale for you." Jessie suddenly held her stomach, just now realizing how hungry she was. "Hey, what do you want to do for dinner? I was thinking we could stop by Mama Melrose's. I'm craving a calzone from there," Jessie said.

"Sure," said Sarah, realizing she was quite hungry as well.

They exited the Apollo theater and stepped into the icy rain pelting at their raincoats and sloshing under their feet. They walked down Bardon Street, which was quite packed with people despite the torrential downpour. It doesn't help that the theater had just let out. Sarah and Jessie looked both ways, then jogged across the street and over to Terrence Lane.

There, nestled in the corner between a bookshop and a café, was a soft glowing neon sign that said *open*. Mama Melrose's didn't look packed or even that busy, but again that could be because the weather wasn't great, and most of the seating at the restaurant was outside.

Sarah and Jessie opened the door to a soft jingle of a bell hanging from the door handle. "Hey, Haddie!" shouted Sarah.

"Hey, ladies! Welcome in. Please grab a seat anywhere you like," Haddie shouted back.

Sarah and Jessie grabbed a corner table toward the back of the restaurant. It was a cozy little place, with only about five tables indoors and bar-like seating but a huge back patio and seating out front. Inside, there were a few tables that led to the kitchen, with a pizza oven blazing that was viewable from the tables. The scent of dough wafted through the air, tantalizing Sarah and Jessie's taste buds. Sarah noticed she started salivating. Maybe she was hungrier than she thought.

"So, ladies, what'll it be today?" asked Haddie, taking out a small notepad and pen.

"I think I'll have the pepperoni calzone," stated Jessie, who also started salivating at the thought of a warm steamy dough pocket stuffed with gooey cheese and spicy pepperoni.

"As for me, I'll take the personal pan pizza with pepperoni, green peppers, and mushrooms. Oh, and a Diet Coke, please," said Sarah.

"No problem, ladies, I'll be right back with your orders," Haddie said.

"So, I'm guessing you absolutely enjoyed the performance today, as evident by the goofy grin on your face," teased Jessie.

"Oh, you have no idea. This was the best birthday gift anyone could have given me," stated Sarah, almost with tears stinging her eyes.

It was Sarah's birthday, and for the most part, it was very low-key, with only a few coworkers wishing her a happy birthday. Sarah didn't mind, though, as she got to spend the day with the person she was closest to, doing the thing she loved most. Sarah and Jessie had been friends for over twenty years, considering themselves to be sisters since they were so close. Sarah couldn't think of a better way to spend her birthday than with an evening at the ballet with Jessie, followed by some delicious piping hot pizza.

"Here you ladies are. One personal pan pizza with pepperoni, green peppers, and mushrooms, and a Diet Coke, and one cheesy, spicy pepperoni calzone," said Haddie.

"Looks delicious, thanks, Haddie," said Sarah.

"Yeah, thanks, Hads," quipped Jessie.

Sarah grabbed a slice of her pizza, a long string of cheese still connected to the rest of it. She took a bite.

"Oof ah hah hot, so hot," breathed Sarah, huffing and puffing, trying to cool down the piece of steaming hot pizza currently burning her mouth.

"Oh, but so delicious," Jessie said, biting into her own steaming hot calzone.

"So," started Jessie, with a knowing grin spreading across her face. "Have you given any more thought to starting an iMatch account?"

"Oh boy, here we go," groaned Sarah.

Jessie had been trying to get Sarah to join iMatch for a few weeks now, constantly pestering her with questions about it. Sarah understood Jessie's intent, trying to help and get her mind off Jake, but Sarah still didn't feel totally ready to get back out there. Sarah and Jake had dated for eight months, and Sarah thought things were going well and progressing at a good speed. That is until Jake decided he liked her coworker better.

That's the problem with dating people at work. Jake ended up breaking it off with Sarah, and to Sarah's surprise, her heart hurt a lot more than she was expecting. It had only been eight months, and it wasn't like they had discussed much of the future together, like getting engaged and married and starting a family, so why did she find herself so down about it?

"C'mon Jessie, you know I haven't yet. I just don't feel ready to get back out there," said Sarah, taking another bite of her food.

Outside, the rain started to slow, now only a drizzle. Inside, Sarah and Jessie finished their food. "Thanks so much, Hads, that was delicious," Jessie said.

"Yeah, that was so good," Sarah said

"It definitely hit the spot," Jessie stated.

"No problem, ladies, thanks for stopping in," replied Haddie.

Sarah and Jessie stood and put on their rain gear and walked out the door. "So, you up for some drinks now, birthday girl?" asked Jessie, nodding over to the direction of the Rootin' Tootin' bar.

"Nah, I think I'm going to pass. I have to get home to feed Rosco and go to sleep as I have an early wake-up call tomorrow for work," replied Sarah.

"Aw boo, okay then, maybe Thursday we can meet up for drinks."

"Sure, I get off work early, so that's perfect." Sarah and Jessie hugged each other and started off in opposite directions. Sarah crossed the street and headed toward home on Delaney Ave.

Sarah lived in a small one-bedroom, one-bathroom condo on the upper eastside of Grenvale, close to the art scene and close to her job as a dance instructor. Her home was cozy, giving off Scandinavian hygge (pronounced hoo-guh) vibes. In the living room was a big comfortable sofa with a pair of cashmere socks on the ottoman and a big plush blanket draped over the back of the sofa.

Across from the sofa was a fireplace with a gorgeous marble mantle. To the left of the living room was the kitchen, with its soft green cabinets and butcher block countertop, with a beautiful bronze faucet and cabinet pulls. To the back of the living room were Sarah's bedroom and bathroom, continuing the warm and cozy vibes.

"Hi Rosco!" exclaimed Sarah. "Oh, you're probably hungry, aren't you, you poor thing?" Rosco was Sarah's American Staffordshire Terrier mix she rescued from the pound a year ago. He was a beautiful brindle boy with white facial markings and white 'socks.'

"Woof woof," Rosco barked, wagging his tail.

Sarah walked over to the pantry and opened it up, grabbing the bag of dog food out. She grabbed Rosco's bowl and poured some food into it. "Here you go, boy. Aww, who's a good boy?" said Sarah, Rosco wagging his tail the entire time.

Chapter 2

It's 5:00 AM, and Sarah's alarm goes off. "Ugh, why is it so early?" groans Sarah as she turns the alarm off. She pulls herself out of bed and heads to the bathroom. Sarah brushes her teeth and her hair and throws it up into a bun. She throws on some workout clothes and walks over to her treadmill. Sarah works out every single morning before work, usually doing thirty minutes on the treadmill, followed by some weighted workouts.

After all, she is a dance instructor and must maintain her physical condition. Sarah throws in her headphones and turns up her workout playlist. After her workout, Sarah heads for the shower, deciding on a full 'everything' shower, including washing and conditioning her hair, washing her body, and shaving. Sarah then throws on her work clothes and heads to the kitchen to make breakfast and feed Rosco.

"What do I want for breakfast today? Waffles? Eggs? Oatmeal?" pondered Sarah. Rosco tilted his head at every word. "You're right, Rosco, oatmeal with berries sounds good."

"Woof," chimed Rosco. Sarah grabbed the oatmeal from the cupboard and poured herself a bowl, then she grabbed the frozen berries from the freezer and poured the mix of blueberries and strawberries on top. Sarah then threw the bowl in the microwave for about a minute. While waiting for her oatmeal to be done, Sarah turned on the TV to the news station. "Let's see what kind of nonsense is going on in the world today Rosco."

The TV reporter was talking, "…and thus denies any wrongdoing. The Grenvale commissioner's office has declined to speak with us so far, but we'll keep trying. That's it from me. I'm SJV News reporter Lucille Bracker. Back to you."

"Thank you, Lucille, and now to the weather with Grant Irashu."

"Thanks, guys. For today's weather, looks like it's more rain in the forecast. Make sure you bring your rain gear with you if you're headed outside today, and now a look at the week's forecast," said Grant.

"Ugh, of course, more rain. That's what I get for living in the Pacific Northwest," griped Sarah.

Although Sarah didn't actually hate the weather, she enjoyed the rainy days most of the time, as it added to her cozy ambiance at home. She just didn't enjoy having to go out in the rainy weather. Plus, the rainy weather made her appreciate her vacations to warm tropical climates so much more. Sarah finished up her oatmeal and grabbed her items, ready to head off to work.

At the corner of Dorey Street and Lance Lane sat the Grenvale Dance Conservatory. It was a two-story building that occupied the corner lot. Sarah had been a dance instructor here for eight years but was previously a dance teacher at another studio for four years before it shut down, the head teacher retiring, leading to Sarah's big move to Grenvale for the position of lead teacher at the Conservatory. Sarah walked up to the building and unlocked it.

Stepping inside, she turned on all the lights and started up the computer. "Let's see what's on the agenda for today," said Sarah looking at the calendar. "We have Ballet I and II today, followed by free dance, then we have interpretive dance and jazz in the evening." Looks like it was going to be a busy day today for Sarah. She always enjoyed these days with multiple dance styles being taught, but of course, her favorite, her passion, was ballet.

Sarah started dancing as a child. She was enrolled in junior ballet and danced all the way through high school and continued on in college. Sarah had big dreams of joining the New York City Ballet Company, and she had well been on her way to doing so, that is until a major injury set her back. Sarah had been in her college ballet company, and they were rehearsing for their big year-end show. It was a production of *Swan Lake,* and Sarah was to be Princess Odette, the young princess who gets turned into a swan by the wicked Von Rothbart.

It was during the *pas de deux,* or the "love duet," between Odette and Prince Siegfried that Sarah sustained a serious injury and could not continue. Much to her dismay, there was to be a scout for the New York City Ballet Company at their performance of Swan Lake. Sarah had to be out of dance for months while healing from her injury. In that time, her skills became less polished, and she knew that she would not make it into the New York City Ballet Company now; it seemed her dream was over.

Once Sarah got healed up and was able to dance again, she started looking for teaching positions, as her second idea for a career was sharing her passion for ballet and dance in general with bright young minds eager to learn.

"Good morning Ms. Shuster," chimed a chorus of children as they trickled in the door.

"Good morning, class," said Sarah. "Ready for a great day of dance?"

Sarah and the kids were prepping for the annual Christmas show, and today was a full rehearsal of it. They only had a few more days to make sure the show was ready before it was performed for the community.

"Ms. Shuster," piped up one of the kids, "I don't like this reindeer costume. Can I be a snowflake instead?"

"No, Jonah, we went over this already. You have to be Donner the Reindeer."

And so on the day went, with rehearsal getting done and the other dance classes being taught. Sarah was wiped out at the end of the day and couldn't wait to get home and order some pad thai take out, have a glass of wine, and relax with some trash reality TV.

Chapter 3

It was finally Thursday, so when Sarah's alarm went off, she was more than eager to get up and get the day started. Because it was Thursday, that meant she got to get off work early. She also had evening plans to meet up with Jessie for some drinks. Sarah got up, exercised, then got ready for work, following the same routine she does every day. Sarah then headed off to work, this time stopping by a coffee shop for a morning cup to help energize her. The coffee shop was called Two Beans and on the way to Sarah's job, so she popped in.

"Welcome to Two Beans," said the barista behind the counter. It was a warm and homey place, with a lot of lounging space inside and a small seating area outside. The smell of coffee and pastries filled the air.

Maybe I'll get a croissant as well, thought Sarah, enticed by the scent and the large pastry display case by the register.

"Hey, welcome in. What'll it be?" asked the barista.

"Let me get a medium caramel macchiato and a croissant, please," said Sarah.

"Sure thing, that'll be eight-fifty."

Sarah grabbed her items and headed off to the Conservatory. The weather was surprisingly pleasant, as in, it wasn't raining for once. It was forty-five degrees out, so Sarah was bundled up in her coat and scarf, the hot coffee warming her hands.

It's a lovely day to be out, thought Sarah as she approached the Conservatory.

It was an easy day at work, as it was a short day, so there weren't many classes to be taught. Ballet III and two private ballet lessons were all that Sarah had on her agenda for the day. It got to be the end of the workday, and Sarah closed up shop, ready to head out and meet Jessie. As she was walking out the door, she bumped into a man.

"Oh my, excuse me," exclaimed Sarah, slight pink blushing her cheeks from the embarrassment of running into a stranger, literally.

"Oh, it's no worries at all," stated the man. Sarah noticed how handsome the man was, very sharply dressed in a blue button-down, khaki pants, and brown dress shoes.

Sarah blushed a little harder. "Are you okay? Again, I am so sorry." Sarah said putting her hands up, wanting to help the man.

"Yes, I'm perfectly fine. It's not a problem at all. You take care and have a good day, ma'am." The man smiled. Sarah nodded and went on her way.

"Sarah!" shouted Jessie, spotting her across the street.

"Hey, Jessie!" Sarah shouted back and crossed the street over to where Jessie was resting against a building.

"How are you, girl? How was work?" said Jessie.

"Oh, you know, same old same old. Work was good. The girls in Ballet III are so talented. It's amazing to watch them," said Sarah.

"Ready to head in and get some drinks?" asked Jessie.

"Let's do it," answered Sarah. They walked into the Rootin' Tootin' bar and were greeted by various neon signs lit up. They walked over to two seats at the bar and sat down. "I'll have a gin and tonic and a plate of fries," said Sarah while Jessie ordered an old-fashioned.

"So…" started Jessie with a knowing grin on her face.

Sarah knew exactly where Jessie was going with this but acted as if she didn't know. "So what?" asked Sarah.

"C'mon, spill the beans, your cheeks are pink, and you have this look on your face," stated Jessie.

"Oh, it's nothing." Sarah said as she took a sip of her drink, the slight bitterness making her pucker her lips ever so slightly.

"C'mon, it must be something," quipped Jessie while taking a sip of her drink.

Sarah sighed. "Ah, if you must know, I was leaving work and literally bumped into a stranger…who just so happened to be a very handsome man." Sarah could feel her cheeks blushing again at the thought of the strapping gentleman she ran in to.

"Oooo and…?" Jessie pushed on.

"And nothing. I bumped into him, apologized, he said it was fine, and we went about our days."

"Hmph, okay, fine then. With that, have you signed up for iMatch yet? Girl, you would get so many hits on it you have nothing to worry about." Jessie said, stealing a fry off of Sarah's plate.

"That's the thing though, Jessie, I don't want 'so many hits.' I want to find one guy who is *the* guy and be done with the dating scene."

Both girls were finishing up their second drinks when a guy across the way offered to buy them each another. Sarah didn't know if it was the alcohol, thinking about the guy she bumped into earlier, or the interest the guy across the bar was showing her, but she started to ponder creating an iMatch account.

"Ugh, okay, fine, if, and that's a big if, I create an iMatch account, I'll need your help to set it up."

Jessie squealed with excitement. "Definitely."

"So, you want to come over then, bake some cookies and set up an iMatch account?" asked Sarah.

"You know it."

The girls closed out their tabs and left the bar, walking toward Sarah's condo on Delaney Ave.

"Hey, Rosco," Jessie said, bending down to receive kisses from the dog and petting his head, Rosco's tail wagging exuberantly.

Sarah also bent down for kisses and petted Rosco's head. Sarah then headed toward the kitchen and pulled some pull-apart cookies out of the fridge. Jessie grabbed a sheet pan and turned the oven on. Then, both of them started placing the cookies on the pan. Sarah also turned up some music. This was definitely a fun girls' night that Sarah needed. Sarah had been so busy recently with the big Christmas performance coming up that she hadn't taken any time for herself to just chill and have some fun.

"Alright, cookies are in the oven. Time to get down to business," said Jessie clapping her hands together.

Sarah groaned. "Ugh, fiiine. Let's get this over with."

Sarah wondered why she was so against creating an iMatch. She could set any parameters she wanted and could turn down any requests she got. It's not like she was locked into having to go on dates with the people who showed up on her profile. Sarah wondered if it was because she was afraid what happened with Jake would happen again. That she would find herself into someone, be on a good forward path with them, then turn around and get her heart broken after investing time, emotions, and money into the relationship.

Jessie could sense Sarah's hesitation and asked her about it. Sarah explained what she was feeling and why she was so hesitant to start dating again. "I don't want to get burned again. You know, like what happened with Jake," said Sarah.

"Aw, Sarah, you can't let that one bad experience dictate your future. As a wise baboon once stated, 'The past can hurt, but you can either run from it or learn from it.'"

"Did you just quote *Disney's The Lion King* to me?" Sarah laughed, "Well, that is some good advice. Not sure it fits my situation, but what a smart baboon."

Sarah and Jessie opened up iMatch on Sarah's computer. The website chimed a little jingle, and a big welcome message appeared across the screen. There were testimonials and a "This is how easy it is to set up" message, followed by a big red sign-up now button. Sarah moved the mouse over the sign up now button, took a shaky breath, and clicked on it.

Up came a form to fill out, asking basic questions like name, age, race, gender orientation, etc. Then it asked her to take a compatibility quiz asking questions like "Where would you most like to live?"

A. In a large city

B. In the suburbs

C. In a small quiet town

D. In a rural area

What are your three main reasons for wanting a relationship?

A. Emotional security

B. Frequent intimacy

C. I want someone to spend my free time with

D. So I'm not alone

What is most likely to make you interested in someone (choose two)?

A. Their career

B. Financial security

C. Warm-heartedness

D. Appearance.

Sarah went through the quiz, answering quickly and with what first came to mind. Finally, she finished her profile by entering her email, choosing her username, and entering a password. *Ding* Sarah's email chimed. She had just received a welcome email from iMatch.

"Alright, well, now we just sit back and wait and let those requests pour in. I'm so proud of you, girl. This will work out for the best. I have a feeling," stated Jessie.

Chapter 4

A few days had gone by, and Sarah had received just a few notifications from iMatch that someone had matched with her. Sarah was feeling a little disappointed, to her surprise, as she was hesitant to create an account in the first place. It did hurt a little bit to think no one wanted to match with her. Of the prospects she did have, she was only interested in two of them. Sarah responded back to the messages: *Hi there! I'd be glad to meet you for some coffee. Just let me know when and where.*

The first guy was Adam Weir, who was a dentist in town. His hobbies included hiking, playing with his dog, scuba diving, and cooking. So far, he seemed like a decent guy to Sarah.

"Well, Rosco, tonight is my first date since…well, in a long time," said Sarah. At least Adam was decent looking, tall with blonde hair and blue eyes, and he was well educated. Sarah picked out a blue floral blouse and a pair of jeans paired with a pair of nude wedges. She threw her golden hair up into a messy bun, put some eyeshadow on that complemented her ocean blue eyes, swiped some mascara on, and finished the look off with coral lipstick. Sarah cleaned up nicely, if she did say so herself.

Sarah left her condo and walked briskly toward Two Beans coffee shop, bundled up in her winter coat. The weather was fairly decent, just overcast and cloudy, with a slight wind blowing. Sarah opened the door, which jingled, and the barista welcomed her in. Sarah scanned over the people sitting enjoying their coffees and pastries until her eyes settled on the man that matched the profile picture on iMatch; well, at least she wasn't catfished. Adam looked very much like his profile picture.

"Adam?" asked Sarah, walking over to the man sitting and reading The Grenvale Times, the local newspaper.

"Ah, you must be Sarah. Please join me," said Adam. Well, at least he was a polite gentleman. That was a good start. "Can I get you something, a coffee perhaps?" asked Adam.

"Sure, I'll take a large latte, please, and a scone; I haven't eaten in a while," replied Sarah. Adam returned with the items.

"So, how about this weather, huh?" asked Sarah, internally groaning. Was that the best she could come up with, the weather? She was quite rusty on this whole dating thing.

"Yes, it's not too bad, luckily, unlike that rain storm the other day." Adam chuckled, taking a sip of his coffee.

"Well, tell me a little bit more about yourself. I know you like hiking, have a dog, and enjoy cooking. Tell me a little bit more about those," Sarah said.

And on did Adam talk; he really *really* enjoyed talking about himself. On he went about his multiple and various hiking trips, traveling around the world to hike in some of the best places: Kungsleden in Sweden, Gotemba Trail in Japan, and Kalalau Trail in the USA. Then he went on about cooking, how he studied with a master chef and thought about going into the culinary profession but had already done all the schooling for dentistry and thus only cooked as a hobby. The only thing Sarah didn't mind was when Adam talked about his dog.

"…and he is still a young pup right now, only a year old, but he's quite big and only going to get bigger. Here, look at these photos of him," Adam went on. At least the dog was a cutie. Sarah didn't mind looking at pictures and would share her own of Rosco if she could get a word in.

"Well he's cute-" Sarah started to say, finishing up her scone.

"I've also been scuba diving in many great places," Adam said, cutting Sarah off. The barista had come by and could tell the date wasn't going well, giving Sarah a look while Adam kept talking. Sarah's cheeks flushed.

"Well, this has been nice," started Sarah, "but it's getting late in the evening, so I should be -"

"Oh yes, just one moment, I have to tell you more about my scuba diving," Adam said cutting Sarah off again. Sarah listened to Adam go on, again. Finally getting a chance to get a word in.

"Well, it's getting late, so I should go"

"Oh yes, of course, not a problem. This was very nice. I'm glad to have met you. Maybe we can do this again," said Adam.

"Maybe," responded Sarah unconvincingly while rising from the table. "I'll call you."

Sarah honestly had no intentions of going back out with Adam. She couldn't stand to listen to him drone on about himself anymore. He was a very nice guy, polite and distinguished, but it just wouldn't work between the two of them. Adam was not what Sarah was looking for.

Chapter 5

A few days passed by since Sarah's not disastrous, but not great date, and she had her next date with one Jonah Lambert coming up. Also coming up was the big Christmas show at her dance studio. It was only two days away.

"Hey, Jessie!" said Sarah on the phone, pacing back and forth in her living room, a fire blazing and hot chocolate cooking on the stovetop.

"Hey, girl! We haven't had a chance to speak yet, give me all the deets. How was your date with…what's his name? Adam?"

"Yes, Adam, and it was, well, a date. He was nice, good looking, he's a dentist and has great hobbies, but he seemed a little full of himself, as in, he wouldn't stop talking about all his hobbies and how great he was at them," Sarah said.

"Aw bummer, well maybe this next date you're going on will be better," said Jessie.

"I don't know if I want to go on that date. My first one did not go well; how do I know this second one will be any better? I don't think I can sit through listening to a man go on about himself again."

"Well, I guess you don't know, but you should still give it a shot, you never know. This next guy could be it for you." Jessie said.

"I suppose so," Sarah sighed.

*****

It was two days later and was the night of the big Christmas show. Sarah had a lot on her mind for the show but hadn't forgotten about Jonah. She had invited him to come and see the show before going out for drinks. Jonah was a contractor, and he had brown hair and brown eyes and was quite muscular, thanks to his job; at least, that's what his profile picture showed. Sarah was at home getting ready, fretting about this and that, hoping for success tonight.

"It's okay, Sarah, you got this. Your students are all very talented and have been practicing. Everything will turn out," said Sarah to herself. *Ding,* her phone chimed.

She looked down to see Jonah had messaged her.

Hey! Good luck with tonight's performance. It'll be great.

Well, that's sweet, Sarah thought.

Sarah made it to the Conservatory, and her students were already waiting for her. A nervous energy filled the air. All the students were chattering amongst themselves.

"Alright, students listen up!" shouted Sarah. "Tonight is a big night, and you all have worked so hard to get here. You're all going to do great. Now, go and break a leg!"

A cacophony of voices sprung up as all the children started hustling and bustling around, getting ready.

"I can't find my antlers!" cried one student.

"Where is my red nose?" cried another.

"Ms. Shuster, my shoes hurt my feet," whined another.

Sarah was running around trying to appease all the students. "Alright, curtains in five minutes, guys, places," said Sarah.

All the young Ballet I and II students lined up on the stage. Out in the sitting area, the lights dimmed, voices hushed, and in the audience was Jonah. The curtain rises, and Christmas music starts to play, starting with "Up on the House Top." On stage, nine little reindeer start their performance. The song comes to an end and the little reindeer take a bow, and exit stage left, except little Rudolph who got confused and went stage right. Next, eight little Christmas trees come out on stage and perform to "Oh Christmas Tree", as soon as the music ends, a few trees run off the stage while the rest take a bow, then exit the stage.

Then, come eight little snowflakes on stage dancing around, and finally, with the little snowflakes still on stage, the girls from Ballet III and the students from summer intensives come out and perform acts from *The Nutcracker,* performing stunning versions of the *Waltz of Flowers* and *Waltz of the Snowflakes*, and two of the schools' top students performing as the Sugar Plum Fairy and Cavalier in the *Pas De Deux*. The music ended and the students on stage took a bow, before disappearing behind the curtain.

The curtain then rises, and all the students line up to take a bow, followed by the curtain closing. There is a standing ovation as the crowd cheers.

Sarah comes out on stage. "Thank you all so much for attending tonight's Christmas performance. All these students worked so very hard on this show, and they're all glad you came out to support them. Remember, there are donation boxes at the back exits. Any little bit helps and goes to support the costumes and shows just like this. Thank you again." Sarah took a bow.

With that, this year's dance season was officially over, and she was on winter break. She had two weeks of no work, no schedules to follow, and no planning of what dances were being done on what day. She could finally take a breath.

After the show, Sarah was walking to meet up with Jonah but got sidelined by other parents and people in the community wanting to talk to her.

"Congratulations on a job well done," said one parent.

"That was a tremendous performance," said another.

Finally, "Hey, Sarah! That was a fantastic performance. Those kids sure are talented," said Jonah. "And they had a great teacher," he added.

"Aw, well, thank you," replied Sarah. "Want to get out of here?"

"Sure, I was thinking we could go to Le Cherie's, so we could get food and drinks. How does that sound?"

"Sounds great," said Sarah, realizing she was starving after the Christmas performance.

Sarah and Jonah walked over to the restaurant from the Conservatory, almost the entire way silent. They walked into the restaurant.

"Two, please," said Jonah. The host led them to a corner booth.

Sarah slid into it while Jonah pulled out the chair and took a seat. Sarah glanced over the menu, knowing she definitely wanted a glass of wine, and she was feeling like having fish tonight.

On the menu was a beautiful-sounding dish of salmon, cured in a dry salt rub and served with a whipped egg yolk mousse and garnished with microgreens. Sarah decided she would have that with a glass of Sauvignon Blanc, as it pairs beautifully with fish, salmon in particular. Jonah decided to go for an old-fashioned and thick-cut pork chop drizzled with a balsamic glaze and served with a baked potato and asparagus.

"So, tell me a little bit more about yourself. I know you had on your profile that your hobbies include skating, playing guitar, and playing video games," Sarah said.

"Oh, yeah, I like to do those things, they're fun" said Jonah, not elaborating any further.

"Well, that's cool. My own hobbies include reading, playing with my dog Rosco, and dancing, although that is also my job, so I don't know if it counts as a hobby." Sarah chuckled.

"Oh, that's cool," said Jonah, again, not elaborating any further. An awkward silence filled the air. Where Adam had talked too much, Jonah did not talk enough. Luckily, the drinks and food had just come out. Sarah took a big sip from her wine glass, the dryness of the wine causing her mouth to slightly pucker.

The night continued on, with Sarah trying to make conversation with Jonah, but Jonah not reciprocating. Only answering in short statements or being very vague.

"Well, tell me about your favorite video game," Sarah said, trying to elicit more than just a few words from Jonah.

"I have a few." Jonah said, again not elaborating. Sarah found herself getting flustered trying to converse with Jonah, almost to the point of frustration, and knew this was not going to work out. There would not be a second date. The waiter came by asking about the check, giving Sarah a look as he had witnessed Sarah struggling with Jonah. Sarah blushed, slightly embarrassed, and asked to split the bill.

"Well, Jonah, this has been an enlightening evening, it was quite nice, and the food was amazing, but I don't think this is going to work between us. I'm sorry," Sarah stated.

Jonah sort of just shrugged. "Hmm, okay then."

Sarah finished paying her portion and stood up.

"Can I walk you home?" asked Jonah, the second most words he's said all night.

"No, thank you, I'll be fine," stated Sarah. With that, Sarah walked out the door.

Chapter 6

A couple days have past, and Sarah received a few more matches on iMatch. However, based on her last two dates, she wasn't feeling very confident in these matches. "Maybe the algorithm is messed up somehow, Rosco. Maybe it's not matching me up correctly. I'll ask Jessie about it when she gets here."

It was time for another girls' night, and so Jessie was coming over later. Sarah also hadn't told Jessie about her last date with Jonah. She couldn't wait to spill the details on that one to her.

There was a knock at Sarah's door. Rosco let out a bark. "Oh, Rosco, you know it's just Jessie, relax." Sarah went to open the door, and Jessie flung herself around Sarah's neck.

"Hey, girl!" exclaimed Jessie.

Sarah laughed. "Hi Jessie, come on in."

Rosco ran over and started sniffing Jessie intently, wagging his tail, knocking a glass off the coffee table in the process. "Oh, Rosco, at least it was just water."

Jessie and Sarah grabbed some paper towels and started to clean up.

"Okay, girl, now tell me all about how your date with Jonah went. I'm dying to know, cause he was a cutie."

"Well, I hate to be the bearer of bad news or disappointment, but there won't be a second date. And honestly, I don't think there will be any other dates, period."

"What? Why?" exclaimed Jessie.

"Well, Jonah, for one, was a man of very, very few words. It was like pulling teeth trying to have a conversation with him. I don't know, I feel like maybe the algorithm is messed up or something, and it's matching me with people who I just don't vibe with."

"Well, you haven't been on it long. You just have to give it a chance. You haven't matched with that many people yet. I still believe Mr. Right is out there somewhere waiting for you."

"Yeah, I suppose you're right," sighed Sarah.

At that moment, Sarah's phone dinged with an alert on iMatch.

"Hey, look! You just got another match. Maybe this will be Mr. Right," said Jessie, all excited now.

Sarah looked at her phone to see the match. "Eh, I don't know about him. He kind of looks like a younger version of my dad. That would be kind of weird to date that."

Jessie sighed. "Oh, Sarah." Sarah broke out a bottle of rosé and turned up some music. "Let's forget about stupid boys and dating and just have fun tonight."

Chapter 7

A few weeks had passed for Sarah. It was a brand-new year, she was back at work, and she was still getting matches on iMatch, but not accepting any of them. At this point, she thought it was definitely something wrong with her and not the app. She couldn't help but think that in the back corners of her mind, Jake was still there, preventing her from truly moving forward into dating and finding a guy.

Jake Leifhour seemed like the perfect guy. He and Sarah worked together, which is how they met, and they hit it off instantly. He was definitely cute, with a sort of puppy dog look about him. They had similar interests, like reading, and often were reading the same book at the same time, then discussing it, sort of like their own mini book club. Sarah felt very comfortable in her relationship with

Jake and, in her own mind, could see herself maybe moving on to the next step with him, although that was never discussed. Then one day, eight months into it, it all crumbled apart when Jake told Sarah he didn't want to be with her anymore and instead was talking to another girl at work, Victoria.

The worst part of it was Jake knew Sarah didn't like Victoria. She was stuck up and snobby and always acted like she was far superior to everyone else, even though she was the newest on the team. So, what exactly did Jake see in her? The good news for Sarah was they both left the Conservatory soon after, so Sarah wouldn't have to deal with seeing them together or seeing them at all.

Ding Sarah's phone chimed. "Oh great, another iMatch notification."

Sarah was just about to decline the match when she gave it a second look and felt something in her gut; he looked oddly familiar too. Something told her to give this guy a chance, don't pass on him. His name was Theodore Caddel, he was thirty-four years old, and he was a paramedic in town. His hobbies included reading, taking care of his homestead, cooking, and playing video games. He was also good-looking. Sarah clicked the match back button. *Ding,* the phone chimed, 'You're a perfect match,' flashed up on the screen.

"Yeah, we'll see about that. I need to call Jessie." Sarah dialed Jessie's number, *ring ring.*

"Hey, you've reached me, Jessie. Sorry I missed your call. Leave a name and message, and I'll get right back to you."

Well, Sarah would have to wait to tell Jessie about this new update in her oh-so-exciting dating life.

Sarah received a message from Theodore: *Hello there, it seems we're a perfect match based on the algorithm. I'd like to test that notion if you wouldn't mind by accompanying me to dinner.*

Well, that's one way to ask a lady out, thought Sarah.

Sarah replied: *I, too, would like to test that notion, put the algorithm to the test. I'd be more than happy to accompany you to dinner. How is next Friday?*

Next Friday is perfect. See you then.

Sarah squealed. She was both nervous and excited at the same time. She didn't know why but something just felt different about this one.

*****

Buzz buzz Sarah's alarm went off, except she set it for the wrong time and was now running late to work. Sarah flew out of bed and ran into the bathroom, quickly brushing her teeth and throwing her hair up in a messy bun. She then quickly got dressed and ran out to the kitchen, where Rosco was waiting by his food bowl. "Aw, I know, boy, your breakfast is a little late today, buddy. I'm sorry," Sarah said while pouring Rosco's food into his bowl.

Now what was Sarah going to have for breakfast? "I need something quick and easy. Oh, I know, I'll have some Eggo waffles with fruit, and I'll bring a yogurt with granola with me to class." Sarah popped two waffles into the toaster oven. Something must've been burned already in there because her house started to smell smoky and burnt.

At least Sarah hoped it was something else and not her breakfast burning. Sarah grabbed the waffles, wrapped them in a paper towel, and flew out her door. She ran down the steps inside her condo and out the front door when *thud*, Sarah went flying to the ground.

Sarah had slipped on an ice patch, twisting and possibly breaking her ankle. "Ow! Ow Ow! Son of bitch," yelled Sarah, holding her ankle, tears coming to her eyes.

A passerby jogged over to see if she was okay. "Oh, hun, you took quite a tumble. Are you okay? Do you need an ambulance?"

"Yes, I think so, I can't move it at all, ow, and it hurts a lot."

The passerby dialed 911, and soon enough, there was an ambulance. If Sarah's situation wasn't embarrassing enough already, all the paramedics that responded were *hot.* One of them walked over to Sarah. He was a strapping lad towering over her as she sat helpless on the ground. He knelt down, and Sarah's heart skipped a beat. He had gorgeous brown hair highlighted with hints of caramel and honey. His eyes were a gorgeous hazel color, a warm golden mix of honey hues and caramels with some green. He had a defined, chiseled jaw. Sarah's eyes then flickered over to the name tag on the man's shirt. *Caddel,* it read.

"Oh no," groaned Sarah.

"Ma'am, are you okay? What's hurting you?" said the man, his voice a mix of equally smooth and comforting notes with a hint of gruffness that could be attributed to his job since it often required straightforward-ness and some sternness. "I'm going to get some information from you for paperwork, starting with your name."

"Sarah…Sarah Shuster," said Sarah with an almost guilty look on her face. The paramedic laughed.

"Well, I thought we would be meeting over dinner; this isn't an ideal circumstance, but, in any case, hello there, I'm Theodore, and I'll be taking care of you today."

"Say, have we met before this and before iMatch? You look awfully familiar," said Sarah.

"You know, I was thinking the same thing. Now that I think of it, you're at the dance school, aren't you? Yeah, you ran into me leaving the building recently."

"Oh, that's right," Sarah said, her cheeks blushing. Sarah's heart was pounding in her chest as the paramedics loaded her into the back of the ambulance. Sarah was surprised at her reaction. She can't be falling like this for some guy she just met; she would only be friends at first, as she had to be to protect her heart. The ambulance drove off to the hospital.

"Oh my gosh, Sarah!" said Jessie, walking into Sarah's hospital room. "What happened? Are you okay?"

"Yeah, just hurt my ankle, is all." Sarah was still blushing from the incident and having Theodore be the one to show up. "So, Jessie, I hadn't had a chance to tell you, but I, uh, have a date planned for Friday…with the paramedic."

Jessie's face lit up, and the biggest grin spread across her face. "No. Way. Tell me everything."

"Well, it's not exactly what you think. We had initially matched on iMatch. It just happens that we met earlier than Friday, thanks to me totally eating it today."

"Ooo, okay, so are you all still on for Friday then, with your ankle and everything?" asked Jessie.

"I'm not sure, I think I'll be up for it, just on crutches, but that doesn't mean I can't still eat and drink."

Friday came, and there was a knock at Sarah's door. She was dressed in a slinky black dress but with Adidas sneakers, as she could only wear one at the moment, and she needed to be comfortable. Her hair was half pulled up, half down. She had some mascara on and a red lip. She was definitely feeling herself today, despite the bum ankle. Theodore was taking her to Le Cherie's, the same place she had her date with Jonah, although Theodore didn't know that. After all, Le Cherie's was the fancy place in town to eat at. Sarah hobbled over to the door, her foot in a medical boot. There was Theodore, standing looking dapper and clean-cut in his all-black suit. Sarah's heart skipped a beat or two, and she caught her breath.

C'mon, Sarah. Get it together, she thought.

"Hello, milady. Are you ready to go?" asked Theodore.

Ah, so he is a gentleman, Sarah thought. "Yes, let me grab my crutches, and we can hobble on out of here." Sarah chuckled, then groaned internally. "Why am I like this?" she pondered quietly to herself. Theodore and Sarah couldn't walk to the restaurant this time due to Sarah's ankle situation, so they took Theodore's black Chevy Silverado pickup truck.

They arrived at the restaurant and walked inside. "Hello, it's a table under the name Caddel."

"Yes, right this way," said the hostess. The restaurant was very nice. It had a French flair about it, sort of like if you were in Paris dining at a fine restaurant there. They even had a long window with a portrait of the Eiffel Tower hanging up, so it looked like you were overlooking it while dining. It was a very elegant place, with white tablecloths and waiters in suits. They also had an extensive wine cellar which Sarah loved. They had some wines that had been aging for years and cost $250 a bottle!

Sarah and Theodore sat down. "Theodore."

"Please, call me Theo, my buds at work all call me Theo, so you can too."

Sarah smiled, then grabbed the menu. "Okay, Theo." She was feeling rather hungry, so she thought about an appetizer. However, she didn't want to appear greedy with ordering if Theo was going to pay.

Luckily, it was as if Theo had read Sarah's mind. "Would you like to share an appetizer?" asked Theo.

"Sure. I was thinking about the—"

"Escargot," they both said at the same time.

"Jinx! You owe me a glass of wine," said Sarah.

"Fair enough," replied Theo. The waiter came to take their orders.

They ordered the escargot, then Sarah ordered the flank steak with garlic and herb compound butter, roasted fingerling potatoes, and a mix of vegetables like carrots and cauliflower. For her drink of choice, Sarah went with a Cabernet Sauvignon, as it pairs nicely with steak.

As for Theo, "I'll have the parmesan herb-crusted rack of lamb with minted green peas and a chianti, please." Ah, so he's sophisticated too.

While they waited for their food, Sarah and Theo started talking. "So Theo, tell me more about your homestead. I'm real interested in hearing about it."

"Well, it's a pretty decent size. It's a couple of acres. I have a cow, two pigs, some goats, chickens, and a cattle dog, named Zoe. I also have a vegetable garden where I grow lettuce, tomatoes, carrots, squash, and zucchini. I would love to get a horse someday too. It just hasn't been the right time yet. That's pretty much all there is to it. But enough about me, how about you? What are your hobbies?"

"Oh, my hobbies pretty much include baking, reading and dance. Although I don't know if that counts as a hobby since it's my job. Oh, and playing with Rosco, my rescue dog."

"I, too, like reading. Are you currently reading anything interesting?"

"Oh, you know, just the classic *Sense and Sensibility* by Jane Austen. Have you read that work?" asked Sarah.

"I wish, as well as everybody else, to be perfectly happy, but, like everybody else, it must be in my own way," said Theo quoting directly from the book. Sarah's jaw about hit the floor. "As I said, I enjoy reading." Theo grinned.

As the night continued, they ate and drank and talked about various things. Sarah was enjoying herself. At the end of the night, Theo drove Sarah back home and walked her up to her condo. "Well, thank you for the wonderful night. I genuinely enjoyed it," said Sarah.

"Yes, me too," said Theo, a brief glint in his eye.

Sarah and Theo were standing just inches away from each other. Sarah could feel Theo's body heat radiating off him and could smell the chianti wine on his breath. Oh, how Sarah wanted to fully lean in and kiss Theo! Theo reached out and touched Sarah's arm, sending electric tingles throughout her body.

"I had a great night. I'll talk to you soon," said Theo, and with that, he walked away, leaving Sarah standing at her door breathless.

Sarah couldn't believe it. She would not let herself fall like this for some guy she just met. No way was that going to happen. No way could it happen. It just couldn't. Sarah had to protect her heart at all costs, and if that meant taking things nice and slow with Theo, then so be it.

Chapter 8

Theo walked into work and was immediately hounded by his squad mates.

"So, how was your date, man?" asked Theo's good buddy Trevor.

"Yeah, man, how was it?" asked another squad mate, who was busy shining his work shoes.

"Guys, relax. It was good. We had a great time." Theo grinned, while grabbing some supplies to refill the ambulance.

"That's it, man? You got nothing else to share?" Trevor asked.

"No, that's it." Theo laughed.

"Do you think you're going to see her again?" Trevor asked, also grabbing some extra items for the ambulance.

"Yes, I'd like to. I'm thinking of inviting her to the Grenvale Festival."

With that, the fire station's alarm went off, meaning they had a call to respond to. Theo donned his gear and climbed into the ambulance, and they drove off.

Meanwhile, across town, Sarah was at work when Jessie came in to visit while Sarah was on break. "So tell me about Mr. Paramedic Man," Jessie said.

"Well, you already know he's a paramedic, oh, and he has his own homestead, and he's very well-read. He even quoted *Sense and Sensibility* to me."

"Are you going to see him again?"

"I'd like to. I'm waiting for him to message me back. I had just texted him that I had a lot of fun the other night and would like to hang out again." Sarah's phone chimed.

Hey, I had a great time too. I'd love to hang out again. Maybe we can go to the Grenvale festival together, said the message from Theo.

Sarah replied: *That sounds lovely. Just let me know what time.*

The Grenvale Festival was a huge community festival put on to celebrate the coming of spring, the official day which is March twentieth, although the festival ran for a whole two weeks. Usually, there were some carnival rides set up, lots of food booths, and artisan craft booths. It was always a fun time, and the money from tickets go back to the Grenvale community service center.

"Guess I'm going on a date at the Grenvale Festival," said Sarah.

"That'll be fun and cute," stated Jessie.

Sarah finished up her work day, which was more difficult now that her ankle was out of commission, and left the building. On her way out, an ambulance drove by, and Sarah wondered if Theo was on it, working. Sarah was on her way to the doctor's office for a check-up of her ankle. She was hoping to get the boot off soon.

"Hi, appointment for Sarah Shuster with Doctor Kleibowitz."

"Yes, please have a seat, and someone will be right with you."

Sarah sat down in the waiting room. It was a rather calming place, with the walls painted a light blue with floral artwork hanging up. They even had a small fountain running and a white noise machine going too. It helped to put patients at ease.

"Ms. Shuster," said the nurse, "right this way."

They checked Sarah's vitals, like blood pressure and pulse, and took her weight. Then the nurse led Sarah to a room and had her sit on the bed, listening to her breathing and heart with the stethoscope.

"Ms. Shuster, hi, how are you doing? How's the ankle?" said Dr. Kleibowitz.

"It's been fine, it hasn't been hurting, really, and I'm very eager to get this boot off."

"Well, let's get an X-ray and see how it's looking, and you might just get that boot off yet."

After a few minutes of waiting after the X-rays, the doctor came back in with the results. "Great news Sarah. The ankle looks great, and we can go ahead and remove the boot. Now, I do want you to be careful with it. I don't recommend putting too much pressure on it just yet. You're clear to go to work, as you've been doing, but I wouldn't do any spins or anything like that on that ankle, okay?"

"You got it, doc." Sarah was relieved to finally have the boot off. Now she wouldn't have to hobble around the festival with Theo.

Sarah thought about messaging Theo, asking him how his day was. *Was that too desperate?* Sarah thought. *Should I just wait until I see him next?*

Sarah messaged Jessie: *Hey, so I sort of want to message Theo, but I don't know if that's desperate looking. Would he think I'm weird or clingy by doing so? I just want to ask him about his day.*

Jessie replied: *Go for it. I don't think it's desperate. I think it's a nice gesture that you're checking up on him.*

Sarah decided to go for it: *Hey Theo, it's Sarah. Just checking in on you and seeing how your day was :)*

Now she just had to wait for a reply. Five minutes went by, then twenty, then forty minutes went by with no response. Sarah was starting to worry she had made a mistake in messaging Theo. Sarah tried to go about her day, not thinking of the message she sent and not focusing on receiving a response back.

*****

It was a few hours later, and Sarah was at home making dinner. Tonight was an easy dinner of some roasted chicken with rice and peas and carrots, with a glass of wine, of course, this time a nice rosé to pair nicely with the chicken. Sarah was just about to sit down on her cozy sofa, with the fire going and Rosco laying in front of it, when her phone dinged. Sarah's heart skipped a beat. Could it be Theo? She looked down at her phone.

Hey! I'm so sorry for the delay in responding. Work was hectic today. We had many patient runs and hospital visits today. I appreciate you checking in on me, though. How was your day?

Sarah realized she was grinning, a tinge of blush on her cheeks. What was this that she was feeling? Sarah wanted to reply back immediately, but she thought that she was too eager and maybe she should give it some time before responding. "Ugh, why is this dating dance so difficult? I much rather put together another Christmas show with all the students than navigate the dating scene." Sarah started to eat her dinner and watch some TV.

After about thirty minutes, she decided to respond back: *Hey, sorry to hear that work was crazy. My day was good, great actually, cause I got my medical boot off finally. Now I'll be prepared to walk around the festival.*

Sarah hit send. *Ding.*

Oh, that's great news. I'm glad to hear it. I can't wait for our festival date.

"*Me either. Well, I'm going to head off to bed, but talk soon?*" replied Sarah

"*Definitely. Goodnight.*"

Sarah was twirling her hair and definitely blushing.

*****

Sarah woke up in the morning, her throat feeling kind of scratchy. "Oh no, am I getting sick? I can't be getting sick. I have a date tomorrow." Sarah knew what would help, a delicious mint herbal tea that Two Beans café brewed. They called it their "medicinal cold and flu tea."

Sarah got dressed, this time comfortably in a pair of sweatpants and a matching sweater, threw her hair up in her usual messy bun and headed out the door. This time bringing Rosco with her so he could get out and enjoy a walk. Two Beans was pet friendly too. Sarah walked over to Two Beans, running into some of her students on the way who were out and about. Sarah was wondering who else she might run into looking the way she did, a little run down and not feeling her best and walking Rosco. Sarah opened the door to Two Beans, the familiar jingle of the bell on the door alerting the barista that she was there.

"Welcome to Two Beans," the barista shouted. Sarah walked in, looking at her phone and not paying attention when *crash*, she walked right into a person.

"Oh, I'm so sorry. Oh my gosh, are you okay?"

Rosco let out a single bark, the person shaking their hands, trying to get the spilled hot coffee off them. Sarah's gaze wandered up when she saw it was none other than Theo Caddel.

"We have to stop meeting like this." Theo laughed. "Are you okay?" he asked.

"Just a little embarrassed, that's all." Her cheeks flushed with pink.

"And who is this?" asked Theo about Rosco.

"This is Rosco, my baby boy. I adopted him a year ago," said Sarah.

"Oh, what a good boy," Theo said, reaching down to pet Rosco's head. "Are you okay? You sound sort of stuffy" Theo asked.

"I think I'm coming down with a cold, so I'm here from some of the medicinal cold and flu tea. Oh, your coffee. I am so sorry, here let me buy you another one," Sarah said.

"Well, I'm sorry to hear that, and nah, don't worry about it. It's all good. I still have some left in my cup. Anyway, I have to run. I'm running late getting back from my break."

"Okay, stay safe out there," said Sarah. Sarah quickly composed herself and walked up to the counter. "Hi, can I get one medicinal cold and flu tea and one pup cup?"

"Sure, that'll be four-fifty."

Sarah paid and walked to the other end of the counter, waiting for her order, her mind still spinning from her encounter with Theo. "Well, Rosco, what did you think of Theo?"

*****

Sarah felt herself getting progressively sicker as the day went on. The scratch in her throat started to turn more into pain, her nose was getting stuffy, and she had developed a cough. "Great, I'm going to have to cancel tomorrow." Sarah pulled out her phone.

Hey Theo, listen, I am so sorry, but I'm going to have to get a rain check on the festival. It seems my cold is getting worse, and I just don't feel good.

Ding, an immediate reply, *Aww, that's a bummer. That's okay, though, the festival runs for two weeks, so maybe you'll feel better by the end of it. Feel better.*

It was the next morning, and Sarah was lounging in bed, feeling rough. She also looked rough with bags under her eyes as she hadn't slept well, her nose was so stuffy she could hardly breathe through it, and she was coughing a lot. Suddenly, there was a knock at her door.

"Who could that be? Jessie maybe? But I haven't told her that I'm sick yet." Sarah thought quietly to herself.

Sarah pulled herself up out of bed. "Just a minute," she called out. She quickly ran to the bathroom to try and put herself together. She went over to the door and opened it and…

"Surprise!" Theo said.

"Theo? What are you doing here?" Sarah asked in disbelief.

"Well, you said you were sick, so I figured you needed some taking care of, and after all, I am a paramedic. Taking care of sick people is what I do. I brought you a medicinal cold and flu tea from Two Beans and some of my grandma's chicken noodle soup. This is like a magical elixir, trust me."

Sarah almost wanted to cry. This was so kind of Theo to do. She couldn't wait to tell Jessie. "Please, come on in," said Sarah, motioning for Theo to enter. Rosco trotted over and started sniffing Theo intently, probably smelling all the animals on him.

"Hey buddy, remember me?" asked Theo to Rosco. "I didn't mean to drop by unannounced," stated Theo. "I just thought this would help you feel better."

"Oh no, this is so sweet. Thank you, I greatly appreciate it."

Sarah took a sip of the tea, getting hints of minty green and peach tea mixed with lemonade, peppermint extract, honey, and lemon slices. Sarah then opened up the container of soup, sipping some of the broth, the warm liquid soothing her throat as it went down. It was probably the most delicious soup she had ever had. She walked to the kitchen to grab a spoon to dig in. Sarah had not had much of an appetite since she had been sick, but there was something warm and comforting about the soup that sparked her appetite. Maybe it really was a magical elixir.

"So Theo, you said this soup is your grandmother's. Did she make it herself, or do you have the recipe?" asked Sarah.

"I made it, actually. I used to cook alongside her all the time growing up, and we made this soup countless times. I could make it in my sleep at this point."

Ah, so he was handsome, and he could cook.

Sarah and Theo sat on the sofa, with the fire going, Rosco at Sarah's feet, talking about various things like books. Sarah was really enjoying Theo's company. She was starting to feel a little bit better; it was probably that magical elixir soup. "Well, I've kept you long enough. You need to get some rest," said Theo, rising up from the sofa.

Sarah felt a twinge of sadness. She hadn't wanted him to leave. "Okay, thank you again so much for stopping by and for bringing me the tea and soup. I truly do appreciate it, and I think I'm starting to feel better."

"Well, you're welcome. And good, I'm glad to hear that. Now get some rest." With that, Theo was out the door, and Sarah was left standing with a gnawing ache in her chest.

Chapter 9

Back on Theo's homestead, he was hard at work taking care of his animals. He had bales of hay in the bed of his truck that he was unloading for the cow and goats. He also unloaded a few pounds of pig feed. Theo had been up since sunrise, hard at work on his little farm before the sun came out. Today was one of the rare days that they got sunshine, but it was due to be springtime.

Theo's buddy Trevor was coming over to hang out and assist Theo in building new stalls for the animals. Theo's goal was to have a full-on barn and stables. He was slowly working toward that. Theo was dressed in a gray tank top and some Wrangler jeans, with his farm boots on, which of course, were much different than his going-out boots. Sweat was already dripping down his muscular arms, even though it was still early morning.

At about 9:30 AM, Trevor showed up, ready to get to work. "Hey Theo!" shouted Trevor.

"Hey, man, just come on around back," responded Theo. Zoe, Theo's cattle dog, ran up and greeted Trevor with intense sniffing.

"Hey there, girl," said Trevor petting Zoe. Theo and Trevor got to work nailing plywood boards and beams together; the stalls for the animals started to take shape. Theo was proud of his homestead. He worked so hard on it to get it to where it was today. Due to his job and the not-so-normal schedule (it wasn't a nine-to-five job, he actually worked twenty-four hours on and forty-eight hours off), he sometimes needed assistance with taking care of his animals and crops. That's where Trevor and Theo's sister Madeline came in.

Madeline was a few years younger than Theo, at twenty-eight years old, and was a teacher in town. Madeline and Theo had always been very close, so when Theo decided to embark on this adventure of homesteading, knowing he would need occasional assistance, he knew he could rely on his sister.

They had met Trevor at work and had been best buds for six years. Trevor and Theo might as well have been brothers. They were so close. Trevor was always teasing Theo, but Theo being cool, calm, and collected, never let it bother him; call it brotherly love. It was important for Theo to have a bud at work like Trevor, someone who understood the frustrations and stresses of the job and could be there during the bad calls. Trevor was always there for Theo. Trevor could say that taking care of Theo's homestead was a hobby of his. Seeing as how Trevor lived in an apartment and didn't have any land for himself, he lived vicariously through Theo in that sense.

"So, have you told Madeline about Sarah yet?" asked Trevor.

"No, it's too early, I think, but I'll tell her soon." Was that a hint of pink in his cheeks beneath his bronzed skin?

"Maybe I'll invite Mads over for dinner and tell her then," stated Theo. Theo pulled out his phone and texted Madeline:

Hey, Mads, want to come over for dinner tonight? I can make Mom's casserole you love so much.

Ding Theo's phone went off:

Sure, of course I'll be there for the casserole, and I guess for you too lol. Trevor and Theo finished up for the day, and Theo had invited Trevor to stay for dinner with him and Madeline, but Trevor had other plans.

Madeline finished her school day and headed over to Theo's. "Hey bro, hi Zoe." Madeline said.

"Hey, Mads." Theo responded.

"So, what's going on? You usually don't invite me over last minute if it's not related to the homestead or you have something to tell me." Man, Madeline was smart. She caught on already.

"How about we get through dinner first, then I'll tell you. By the way, how's the wedding planning going?" asked Theo.

"It's going well. We're just about done with everything, now just waiting for the big day," responded Madeline.

Theo stood in his kitchen. The interior of his home had an industrial feel to it. His kitchen had an exposed brick wall, with dark blue cabinets and a butcher block countertop. Leading out of the living room, there was a brown leather sofa and a deep wood coffee table with metal accents. Deep rich woods and metal accents spotted the house. To the left was a bookshelf filled with classics like *To Kill a Mockingbird, The Great Gatsby,* and *1984.* Theo took out some chicken to prepare the chicken casserole. He started chopping some onion and celery. Then he grabbed a pot and put water in it to boil for the noodles. Madeline was almost drooling, waiting for the dish.

After baking for twenty-five minutes, the casserole was done. Theo and Madeline dove in, the casserole steaming.

"Okay," said Madeline with a mouth full of food. "What do you have for me? Do you need me to work your farm or something?"

"No, although I appreciate the offer. No, actually, what I wanted to tell you, is that I…well, you see…there may be…a girl," said Theo sheepishly.

"OOO, NO WAY. OH MY GOSH, THEO!" Madeline squealed with excitement.

"See, I knew you were going to act like this. I told Trevor I should have waited to tell you."

"Tell. Me. Everything. What's her name, what does she look like, what does she do? I want to hear it all."

"Woah, easy there, one thing at a time. I promise I'll get to all of it. Her name is Sarah Shuster, and she's the lead dance teacher at the Grenvale Conservatory. She's really smart, well-read, she has a cute dog named Rosco, and dance is her passion. She's also beautiful, with long golden hair the color of wheat and deep ocean blue eyes."

"I see. Sounds like someone is in love. I see that twinkle in your eye when you talk about her."

"I—no, that's not it, not yet anyway. We're just friends right now who are dating. Nothing serious yet."

"But you want it to be?" asked Madeline.

"Maybe," responded Theo.

Chapter 10

It was March twenty-sixth, with only one day left in the Grenvale Festival, and Sarah was feeling much better. So much so that she was going to get to go on her date with Theo. It was a nice day out, with the temperature being seventy-two degrees and some sun peeking through the clouds.

Sarah wore a blue flowy cotton floral knee-length dress with off-the-shoulder sleeves, as she wanted something that evoked spring. She paired it with a pair of brown combat boots. Sarah left her house and walked toward the community center, where she was going to meet Theo. As Sarah was strolling up, she saw Theo standing at the community center holding what she presumed were two cups of coffee.

"Have a caffeine addiction with the two coffees?" joked Sarah.

"Haha, well, with my schedule and the work I do…no, I'm kidding, this one is for you," said Theo back. Theo handed her the cup of warm coffee, and she took a sip. It was a hazelnut latte, one of her favorites.

Theo and Sarah strolled up and down, looking at the artisan booths. There were so many wonderful handcrafted items and other little trinkets to buy. The smell of food wafted through the air. There was pizza, hot dogs, burgers, and funnel cakes available, and a special treat, deep-fried Oreos. There were also caramel apples and cotton candy. At the end of the lane, there was a Ferris wheel.

"Want to go up on that?" Theo asked.

"Um," said Sarah, "I'm not very big on heights."

"Okay, well, maybe later, you can think about it and decide. Besides, it's much prettier at night."

Theo and Sarah strolled around some more, grabbing a bite to eat and enjoying the festivities. Soon night fell, and Sarah was still thinking about the Ferris wheel and whether she would go up on it or not. It was a good opportunity to be close to Theo, Sarah thought.

"Hey Theo, I think I'm ready. Let's go on the Ferris wheel."

"Are you sure? If you're afraid, we don't have to."

"No, it's okay. I want to see Grenvale from up above and see if it's as pretty as you say." Sarah and Theo walked up to the Ferris wheel, Sarah's heart started thumping in her chest, and her palms started to sweat. Why did she put herself in these positions? They were next to the board, and Sarah almost froze in place.

"Hey, you'll be okay. I'm right here with you," whispered Theo to Sarah.

Somehow, the smoothness of his voice caused her feet to unglue themselves, and she walked onto the Ferris wheel. As soon as the ride started going up, she immediately grabbed onto Theo's arm, gripping it tightly. Theo rested his other hand on hers, and her grip softened.

"There, there," Theo said, "it's okay, you'll be alright."

Sarah wondered if this is how all his patients felt; scared of their situation but soothed and calmed by him. Any patient was lucky to have Theo treating them. Sarah mustered up the courage to look out over the town when they reached the top of the ride.

Theo was right. It is absolutely stunning up here, Sarah thought.

Theo, meanwhile, was gazing at Sarah, taken by how beautiful she looked in the lights. Sarah could feel Theo's gaze upon her, and her eyes drifted until she met his. They locked eyes only briefly for a moment before looking away, Sarah's cheeks felt a rush of warmth, and she was sure she was blushing. Luckily, it was dark enough that she didn't think Theo could tell. Little did Sarah know, Theo, too, felt a rush of warmth in his cheeks. Soon enough, they had made their way around and were back on the ground.

"That was incredible, really. The views up there were something else. You weren't kidding," said Sarah.

Yes, the views were incredible, thought Theo, but he wasn't talking about the town views.

"Can I walk you home?" asked Theo.

"Sure, that would be lovely." They strolled down the street and toward her place on Delaney Ave. Once they got to Sarah's place, Sarah invited Theo up.

"I'd love to, but I got to get home, I work tomorrow, and I'm on for twenty-four hours," said Theo. "I'll be sure to message you, though." Theo reached out and gently squeezed Sarah's arm, a twinkle in his eye. "Goodnight, Sarah." With that, he was gone, and Sarah felt the growing familiar gnawing ache in her chest whenever

Theo left. Sarah walked into her apartment, where Rosco was waiting.

"Hey, boy," Sarah said, patting him on the head. "How was my date, you ask? It was fine." Rosco looked at her with his head tilted. "Okay, it was more than fine. It was great. Theo is so thoughtful and kind and genuine and funny, literally all the great attributes." Sarah got ready for bed, thinking about her night. She was falling hard and fast.

Two days later, Sarah woke up to a text, "Good morning! I was wondering if you wanted to come check out the homestead today? Let me know if that works for you." The message was from Theo. Sarah felt a burst of excitement rush through her. She would love to. However, she had work today…but she could play hooky, couldn't she? Sarah called her coworker Jade and let her know she wouldn't be coming in today. Sarah then replied back to Theo:

Hey, good morning. I would love to come over and see your little farm. I don't know if you know this, but I love cows, goats, and pigs :)

Sarah got up out of bed and went to get ready. Today's outfit consisted of a pair of jeans, a green checkered flannel shirt, and hiking boots. Just in case she was going to do any labor on the farm. She then put on a baseball cap and grabbed her sunglasses. She then got Rosco's breakfast ready and headed out the door.

Sarah pulled off onto a dirt road that was quite bumpy. She wasn't sure if her little red Nissan Versa would make it. As she went down the drive, she noticed how peaceful it seemed. It was quiet, with trees lining the drive on one side and an open field on the other. As she approached the house, it looked like a big log cabin. Sarah was both impressed and amused. So this is where and how Theo lived. As she pulled in, she noticed two other people standing with Theo, the sight of Theo sending her heart skipping a beat, and with them was Zoe. As Sarah got out, Trevor let out a whistle, and Theo smacked him on the arm. Madeline just chuckled.

"Hey, Sarah!" Theo said. "This is my good buddy Trevor and my little sister Madeline."

"Not so little sister, thank you very much," Madeline responded. "And this little lady is Zoe. She's my cattle dog."

"Hi, Zoe," said Sarah, petting her head.

Madeline then held her hand out, "Hi, Sarah, Madeline, it's nice to meet you."

Trevor then extended his hand as well. "Hey, Trevor. Nice to meet you."

"So, this is it, huh?" asked Sarah.

"What, not enough for you?" quipped Theo.

"I'll have you know I'm playing hooky from work just to be here, so I expected it to be grand. So far, I am not disappointed," quipped Sarah right back.

"Well, if you don't mind some physical activity, we can start by feeding the animals. With the four of us, it should take us no time at all," Theo stated.

"Sure, I'd love to meet the animals and feed them."

The four of them walked around back to the stall and pen where the goats and pigs were. The cow was out in the field.

"So here we have Bonnie and Clyde, and Ringo and Starr. These are the goats. Then over here, we have Cris P. Bacon and Delilah, the pigs." Sarah stared in bewilderment. "You did not name your poor pig crispy bacon."

Trevor and Madeline laughed. "Yes, that's Theo for you," Madeline said.

"Hey Trevor, come around with me and help me with the bales of hay in my truck. Ladies, you can start feeding the pigs if you don't mind," said Theo. The boys walked off, leaving Sarah alone with Madeline.

"So, Madeline, what is it that you do?" Sarah asked while they walked over to the feed bags.

"Oh, I'm a teacher at Grenvale elementary school. I hear from Theo you're a dance teacher?"

"Yes, at Grenvale Conservatory."

The ladies continued feeding the pigs. Meanwhile, Trevor and Theo were loading up the truck with hay bales. "So, Trev, first impressions of Sarah?"

"Well, she is beautiful, I will say that much. She also seems nice, but I haven't had the chance to talk to her much yet."

"Well, be on your best behavior. None of your funny business, okay? We don't want to go scaring her off."

The men got in the truck and drove around back, where Madeline and Sarah were talking. It looks like they were hitting it off really well. Theo and Trevor let out the hay bales for Lilly, the cow, then all four of them headed inside.

Theo had bought burgers for the night and was going to cook them out on the grill. "Sarah, would you stay for dinner?" asked Theo.

"Oh yes, please do stay," said Madeline.

"Sure, what are we having," responded Sarah.

"Burgers, if that's okay," Theo said.

"Yum, I love a good cheeseburger." Theo started up the grill while Trevor started up the fire pit. The ladies grabbed the cooler from inside the house and brought it outside.

While inside the house, Sarah noticed how clean and simple it was, with not a lot of décor cluttering up the space. She also caught sight of his impressive bookshelf. It was almost enough to make her jealous.

"Did he actually read all these books?" Sarah thought to herself.

Back outside, the girls were gathered around the fire, drinking beers, while Theo and Trevor were manning the grill. Sarah and Madeline were deep in conversation about teaching techniques and exchanging tips and tricks. Sarah liked Madeline. Theo, watching this exchange happen, was delighted.

It was important for his baby sister to get along with his…what did he call Sarah? Surely not girlfriend, not yet anyway. Were they boyfriend and girlfriend? It wasn't made official.

"Dinner's ready," called Theo.

Sarah stood up and walked over to the grill. "These look delicious, Theo."

"Eh, they look alright," teased Madeline. Sarah liked her burger with cheese, lettuce, onion, ketchup, and mustard. Theo liked his with only the patty and the bun, no condiments. They sat around the fire and began to eat.

"Mmm, this is delicious," said Sarah.

"Yeah, man, they're really good," said Trevor. As the night went on, there was pleasant conversation all around. Sarah was enjoying her time. Madeline then brought out dessert, s'mores. Sarah grabbed a skewer and marshmallow and held it over the flames until it got a little burnt and caught fire. Sarah liked her marshmallows a little burnt. She quickly blew out the flames, then sandwiched her marshmallow between two graham crackers and a piece of chocolate. S'mores were also one of Sarah's favorite things to make. Sarah took a bite and pulled the ooey, gooey marshmallow, the marshmallow, and chocolate, making a mess on her face.

"You, uh, have something on your face," Theo said, pointing toward Sarah's chin. "Here, let me help you." He brushed his thumb across her chin. His touch sending shivers down Sarah's spine.

"Thank you," Sarah said sheepishly. She was starting to feel warm, her armpits sweating, and not because of the fire.

"Well, I better get going. I must be up early for work tomorrow. I had a fabulous time tonight. I quite enjoyed myself. Thank you. It was great meeting you, Madeline and Trevor," said Sarah.

"Oh, it was so nice to meet you," said Madeline.

"It was a pleasure meeting you," stated Trevor, extending his hand out for a shake.

"Here, let me walk you to your car," said Theo, placing his hand on Sarah's back. Sarah and Theo started toward the driveway.

"You know, when I was inside your house, I saw your book collection. That's very impressive, I must say."

"Well, thank you. As I've said before, I like to read and write, too."

"Oh, you write? What kinds of things?" Sarah said as she and Theo continued walking to her car.

"Mainly poetry, but I've also dabbled in a novel here and there."

Sarah felt weak in the knees, and was she breathing faster? The weather was beautiful, there was a completely clear sky, and since the property was so big and somewhat removed from town, you could see so many stars in the sky. It was quite a romantic night. They finally reached Sarah's car, standing inches from each other, Sarah had goosebumps on her arms, and she didn't know if they were from the chill in the air or from Theo. Sarah looked captivating under the moonlight, her big blue eyes bouncing the light.

"I enjoyed tonight," said Sarah. "It was great meeting your sister and friend."

"It looks like you guys hit it off well. I'm glad."

"Well, I guess I should be going now." Sarah paused, looking up at Theo. Theo took a step closer, now standing toe to toe. He reached up and tucked a piece of her hair behind her ear. Sarah's breathing quickened, her heart pounding in her chest. Theo leaned in, and Sarah closed her eyes, ready for what was about to happen.

"Theo!" Trevor called out.

Sarah's eyes flew open, and Theo took a step back. Both turned to the source of the yell.

"Theo! Lilly got out!" Trevor yelled.

"Oh no, your cow got out of the pasture?" asked Sarah, still shaking because of what just transpired.

"She does that from time to time, it's a bit of a problem, but we'll manage. I guess I should go take care of that."

"Mmhmm, yes, you probably should, and I'll just head out. Thanks again for everything."

Sarah got into her car and drove off, both of them wondering what had just happened.

Chapter 11

It was 5:00 AM, Sarah's normal wake-up time for work. She did her usual morning routine, including her exercise, and headed to the kitchen to feed Rosco and make herself breakfast. She turned on the TV to the news. Sarah tried distracting herself, but she couldn't get out of her head last night. She had almost kissed Theodore Caddel. Sarah finished breakfast and headed to work. The entire time at work, her mind was distracted, and she couldn't stop thinking about Theo.

It must've been apparent because her coworker asked her, "Who's the guy?"

"What?" replied Sarah.

"You have this dreamy look on your face, so it must be a guy," replied the coworker.

"Well, if you must know, his name is Theodore Caddel, and he's a paramedic here in town."

"How sexy," said the coworker.

Sarah blushed. Sarah couldn't wait for the workday to be over, as she was meeting with Jessie after. She hadn't had a chance to talk to her about what had happened.

Sarah left the Conservatory and headed for the Rootin' Tootin' bar, their go-to for drinks. While walking over, her phone dinged. It was a message from Theo. *Hey, just checking in to see how your day was, how work went.*

Sarah smiled to herself.

Hey! Work was great, the students performed really well. How about you? How was work?

Tough. We had some hard calls today.

Oh, I'm sorry to hear that. Do you want to talk about it?

Sarah genuinely cared about Theo and his rough day. *No, that's okay. I'll be fine, thank you, though.*

Sarah had made it to the bar where Jessie was waiting. "Hey Jessie, man, it's been a while since we actually got to talk and hang out."

"I know, I've been real busy, and I guess you have been too, with a certain Theo, maybe," Jessie said, grinning.

"Do I have a story for you," Sarah said. Sarah took a seat next to Jessie, and they ordered their drinks. A classic cosmopolitan for Sarah and a Negroni for Jessie. Sarah then went into detail about her day at Theo's homestead, how she helped out with feeding, met Theo's friend Trevor and sister Madeline, and had almost kissed Theo, only to be interrupted by a wayward cow. Jessie was smiling so big. Her smile stretched from ear to ear.

"I can't believe that happened to you. What a rough go," said Jessie, almost not believing what Sarah had said. "So, you still haven't kissed him?"

"No," sighed Sarah. After all, they were only friends who were dating, right?

"What do you think your next date will be?" asked Jessie.

"I'm not sure, Theo texted me while I was on my way over here just asking about my day, but he hasn't asked me out again just yet."

"Well, why don't you come up with something and invite him instead?"

"That's a good idea. What can we do?" pondered Sarah out loud. Sarah then got an idea and messaged Theo:

I would like to hang out with you again. Maybe we can go for a hike?

Theo responded back almost immediately: *Sure, that sounds fun. When were you thinking?*

Sarah had a pretty busy week ahead of her, so she planned for the following week, which meant she'd have to wait that long to see Theo.

Sounds like a plan.

*****

A few days later, at work, Sarah was working with the students from the intensive class when one of them passed out. "Oh my gosh, Jules, are you okay? Can you hear me?" asked Sarah, fanning the student as she lay on the ground. "I'm going to call for an ambulance."

"911, what is the location of your emergency?"

"It's the Grenvale Conservatory at the corner of Dorey Street and Lance Lane," Sarah said while still fanning the student.

"Tell me exactly what happened."

"I had a student pass out. I think she got overheated or is dehydrated."

"I already have help on the way. Stay on the phone, and I'll tell you exactly what to do next."

Within minutes, an ambulance appeared, and Trevor and Theo got out. Sarah's heart skipped a beat at the sight of Theo in his work uniform, but she kept her focus on her student. Theo and Trevor walked in and started attending to the girl right away. Sarah got to see Theo in action, and she had been right. He was cool, calm, and collected and provided a sense of comfort to his patients.

Theo had briefly locked eyes with Sarah and said hello, then proceeded to ask her questions to fill out the paperwork; he was very professional. That just made Sarah fall even more. They loaded the girl up in the back of the ambulance to take her to the hospital as a precaution. Sarah would follow and go to the hospital to be with her student until her parents got there.

While at the hospital, Sarah received a message from Theo: *Hey, sorry I didn't interact with you much. I just take my job seriously and didn't want to appear unprofessional. It was great seeing you, though. You looked beautiful.*

Sarah responded: *Thank you and don't worry about it. I totally get it. My student's health and safety was a first priority for me, but I did enjoy seeing you work. It was interesting to see your job in action.*

A few days had passed, and Sarah did her normal routine. Wake up, exercise, go to work. Every single day. Sprinkled into her days were messages back and forth with

Theo. That's what Sarah looked forward to most every single day: the text messages from Theo.

Usually, they just talked about their days, Theo on occasion talking about the stresses of his job and the difficult calls he had. Sarah was glad she could be there for him, a listening ear for his vents, concerns, and anything else he had to say. Sarah also was glad she had someone she could talk to, someone besides Jessie. Not that there was anything wrong with Jessie. It was just nice to have another avenue available, and this one was cute.

Chapter 12

It was the following week, and it was time for Sarah's hiking date with Theo. Sarah put on her leggings, her flannel shirt, and her hiking boots and threw a ball cap on her head. Theo was coming to pick her up in his truck, so they could drive up to the mountain pass. The trail they were hiking was the Giamonte Trail. It was an easy trail, and the views from it were stunning. Soon, there was a knock on Sarah's door, Sarah walked over to open it, and there was Theo, dressed in beige outdoorsy cargo pants and a blue T-shirt, and hiking boots.

"You ready to go?" asked Theo.

"Sure, say what if we bring Rosco? I think he would love being out on the trail, if you don't mind."

"No, of course not, that's a great idea. Hey buddy," said Theo bending down to pet Rosco.

"Okay, let me get him ready. Just a sec," said Sarah as she grabbed Rosco's harness and leash and put it on him. They headed down to Theo's truck, Sarah opening the back door to let Rosco in, with Sarah climbing up into the front passenger seat.

"Alright, everyone good and ready to go?" asked Theo.

"Let's do this," replied Sarah. Sarah was excited. She would get some one-on-one time with Theo out in nature. She wondered if this adventure would end in a kiss.

It was about a forty-five-minute drive to the trail, Theo and Sarah laughing and singing their hearts out to the radio as they drove. Theo rested his right hand on Sarah's thigh, sending electric tingles through her. Rosco had his head out the window, enjoying the wind in his face. Soon, they reached the parking area and pulled in. There were only a few other cars, so the trail shouldn't be busy. Sarah and Theo got out, and Sarah grabbed Rosco from the back, Rosco's tail wagging as he sniffed around.

"There are so many scents for you to sniff here, boy," said Sarah.

The three of them started off down the trail. The weather was beautiful, as it was a gorgeous spring day, seventy degrees and sunny. The views, of course, were incredible. You could see the mountains for miles.

"We should have packed a picnic," stated Sarah, realizing she was probably going to be hungry soon.

"You're right. I didn't even think of that. I'm sorry," said Theo.

As they walked on, Sarah's and Theo's hands brushed up against each other, when finally, Theo grabbed Sarah's hand. Sarah felt the familiar warmth in her cheeks and knew they were red. Sarah grasped Theo's hand back and smiled. Finally, they were getting somewhere. They walked in silence but hand in hand for a bit, with Rosco ahead of them, sniffing just about everything and anything.

Finally, Theo broke the silence. "So, Sarah, I think you know this, but I like you a lot. You're so kind, funny, beautiful, and intelligent. I would like to make us official. Would you be my girlfriend?"

And in that moment, Sarah felt all different kinds of emotions. Elation, confusion, fear. She was thrilled and beyond happy that Theo finally asked her, but she also was afraid of the commitment. Look what happened last time she was someone's girlfriend. Sarah was confused, her heart wanted to say yes, but her mind told her to think it through.

Theo could sense the hesitation in Sarah and said, "Look, I know you've been burned before, and it's scary venturing into something new, but I promise I won't hurt you. You just have to trust me."

Did Sarah trust Theo? Could Sarah learn to trust again? Boy, did Sarah wish she could call Jessie in this moment and talk it through with her. Sarah took a big deep breath in and let it out.

"I like you a lot, too, Theo. You're so well-read, have an admirable job, you're kind, intelligent, and funny. You're right, I have been burned before, and it hurt. It took a while for my heart to heal. It's very fragile. My heart is tugging, saying yes when my head is saying wait. Ultimately though, I have decided that yes, I will be your girlfriend."

In that moment, Rosco ran around both of them, pushing them close together with the leash, bodies touching.

"Rosco!" Sarah said. Sarah could feel Theo's body heat radiating off of him. She looked into his beautiful hazel eyes.

Theo moved his head toward Sarah's, Sarah closed her eyes, and Theo's lips landed on Sarah's. Sarah's world started to spin, and she felt weak in the knees. She kissed

Theo back intensely. She had wanted nothing more than to kiss Theo, and it finally happened. Rosco ran the other way and unbound them, Theo took a step back, and Sarah opened her eyes. "Wow," she said breathlessly.

Wow, was that all I could come up with? She thought.

"Wow, is right," responded Theo, grinning. "What do you say we get out of here and go get some dinner?"

Sarah and Theo headed back to Theo's truck, hand in hand, Sarah smiling from ear to ear. She was happy. They first stopped by Theo's place to get cleaned up and changed. Theo changed into a blue button-down shirt with khaki pants and brown dress shoes, and Sarah had brought a floral dress with her to change into.

Sarah and Theo had a great time at dinner. They had gone to their favorite, Le Cherie's. Sarah had ordered the fresh catch fish of the day with roasted fingerling potatoes and roasted carrots, and Theo ordered the sirloin steak, medium doneness, with a side of mashed potatoes and corn.

After dinner, Theo then drove Sarah back to her condo afterward and walked her up to her door, there, giving her a kiss goodnight. Sarah was on cloud nine. Inside, she talked to Rosco.

"Oh buddy, Theo is a dream come true. He truly is so great. I can't believe I almost passed on him on iMatch. Imagine if I didn't follow my gut." Rosco let out a whine.

"I know, boy, you like him too." Sarah then got ready for bed, as she had work in the morning.

*****

It was the next morning, and Sarah went to work. She had been going about her day when suddenly…

"Sarah! Did you hear?" her coworker Jade exclaimed.

"Hear what? I've been sort of busy working," Sarah responded.

"Girl. THE New York City School of American Ballet is hiring a teacher! It's your dream job!"

"What? The New York City School of American Ballet is hiring?" Sarah asked slightly puzzled.

"Yes, that's what I just said."

"That's amazing. Where did you hear about it?"

"I saw it online."

"I have to check it out. Oh my gosh."

Sarah realized she was shaking. Sarah went to the computer and looked it up, and there it was:

HIRING: 1 EXPERIENCED DANCE PROFESSIONAL MUST HAVE AT LEAST 5 YEARS OF DANCE EXPERIENCE IN BALLET PREFERRED AT LEAST 3 YEARS OF TEACHING EXPERIENCE
OPEN UNTIL JUNE 1st

This was Sarah's big dream. If she couldn't dance in, and be a part of, the New York City Ballet Company, she could take her passion for ballet and her experience teaching, and work at the world-renowned New York City School of American Ballet. Sarah had time to think about it. After all, that was a big decision to have to pack up and leave Grenvale and move to NYC. And what about Theo?

"Oh, Theo! What am I going to do about us and the job? I need to text Jessie," Sarah thought.

Sarah messaged Jessie: *SOS Emergency, we need to talk.*

Jessie immediately replied: *I'll be over at your place as soon as you're done with work.*

Sarah got home from work and had just finished changing her clothes when Jessie knocked on the door. "What's the big emergency?" Jessie asked. "Hello to you too, first off, and secondly, my dream position just opened up."

"What dream position?" Jessie asked pushing her way into Sarah's condo.

"Teacher at the New York City School of American Ballet." Sarah said stepping out of Jessie's way.

"Oh my gosh, Sarah, that's so exciting! So did you apply for it?"

"No, it's open until June 1st. I don't know what to do. On the one hand, it is my dream job, but that means I would have to leave here, leave the Conservatory, leave you, and leave Theo." Sarah said sitting down on the sofa, pulling her feet up under her.

"Oh, right. Well, that's a pretty big decision. Have you told Theo yet?" Jessie asked.

"No, I don't want to ruin what we have. After all, we just made it official."

"Wait, what? You didn't tell me that!" Jessie quipped while gently smacking Sarah in the arm.

"Sorry, yes, the other day on our hike, he asked me to be his girlfriend, and we kissed each other with help from Rosco." Sarah laughed.

"Oh, Sarah, I'd hate to be in your position right now."

"Well, I'd rather not think about that right now, and get on with girls' night, say do you just want to spend the night?"

"Sure, that'll be fun, thanks."

Sarah and Jessie had a fun girls' night. They painted each other's nails, talked and gossiped about different things, ate ice cream from the tub, and drank wine. Sarah tried to keep her mind off the big decision she had to make and when she would tell Theo, but it was gnawing at the back of her mind. After all, Theo couldn't come with her to New York, right? He had his job and homestead here in Grenvale. Maybe they could do long distance? Sarah knew she probably wouldn't sleep tonight with the decisions bouncing around in her head.

The next day Sarah was meeting Theo for bowling. They had been going strong, hanging out every chance they got on days when Theo wasn't working.

"Hey babe," said Theo picking up Sarah, noticing she was a little distant, as if her mind was somewhere else.

"Oh, hey," replied Sarah, distracted by her big decision and telling Theo about New York.

Maybe I won't tell him just yet. I don't want to ruin what we have. What if he's not up for a long-distance relationship? And I won't ask him to give up what he has here to come with me, thought Sarah.

"What's wrong, darling?" asked Theo, sensing Sarah's discomfort and hesitation.

"Oh, it's nothing, don't worry about it, I'm fine," said Sarah.

"Okay, if you're sure, but you know I'm here for you if you need to talk or vent or whatever."

"Oh, I know, thank you."

They arrived at the bowling alley, and Sarah was pretty excited, for she hadn't been bowling in a long time. Sarah considered herself to be quite good at bowling, not even needing to use the bumpers. While there, they ran into Haddie. "Hey, Hads!" shouted Sarah.

"Hey, Sarah!" Haddie shouted back.

"Man, Theo, we haven't gone to Mama Melrose's! That's one place we definitely need to pop into. Haddie, this is Theo."

"Hi, Theo. I think I've seen you around before. You're a paramedic, right? I've delivered pizzas to the fire station before, and you were there."

"That's right, it was some of the best, most delicious pizza I've ever had," stated Theo.

"Well, if you two want, you can stop by Mama Melrose's, and I'll give you a buy one get one free entrée."

"Well, that's so kind of you, thank you," said Theo.

"Yes, Thank you," Sarah said. Theo and Sarah then went about their bowl game, Sarah getting two strikes and Theo getting gutter balls. Sarah laughed at Theo's attempts at bowling.

Okay, maybe he isn't perfect, thought Sarah jokingly.

After bowling, Sarah and Theo took Haddie up on her offer and stopped by Mama Melrose's. While there, Sarah got her usual pizza with pepperoni, mushrooms, and green peppers, and Theo got a pizza with ham, pepperoni, and mushrooms.

"So, Sarah darling, I wanted to ask you for a favor. I work tomorrow, so would you mind coming over to my house and assisting my sister with taking care of the farm."

"Sure, I didn't have any other plans for my Saturday. I'd love to come help out."

*****

After they had finished eating, Theo drove Sarah home.

"Do you want to come up?" Sarah asked.

"Sure, I'd love to," said Theo.

"I know you have to work tomorrow, so you don't have to stay long."

"Staying with you is worth being tired tomorrow. I'll just load up on the caffeine."

They walked up into her condo. Sarah went and got the fire started in her fireplace, she poured two glasses of wine, and then Sarah and Theo sat on the sofa. Theo put his arm around Sarah, and Sarah melted into Theo's chest. Then Theo gently grabbed Sarah's chin and pulled her face close to his. Sarah closed her eyes, and Theo pressed his lips against hers. This was perfect, according to Sarah. She didn't want the moment to end. Theo and Sarah sat on the sofa snuggling in front of the fireplace and drank their wine.

After some time, Theo said, "It's getting late. I probably should get going."

"Aww, okay," replied Sarah, saddened that Theo had to leave.

Theo gave her one last kiss goodbye and was out the door. Sarah felt a pain in her chest grow. Was it because Theo had left, or because she had a decision to make, which was between her dream job and her dream man.

Chapter 13

It was Saturday morning, and Sarah was up bright and early, ready to go to Theo's homestead and help Madeline out. Sarah was a little nervous, she wasn't sure why. Maybe it was because she would be alone with Theo's sister. Did Madeline like her? They seemed to have gotten along just fine the last time they met. Maybe Sarah could find out more about Theo.

Sarah headed toward the homestead, more sure this time her little Versa would be able to make it. Madeline's Jeep was already parked when she pulled up. Sara got out and was greeted by Madeline.

"Hi Sarah!" said Madeline leaning in to give Sarah a hug.

"Hi, Madeline," said Sarah.

"Ready to get dirty? We're not just feeding the animals today. We're cleaning out the stalls."

"Yeah, sure, I'm ready for any kind of work that needs to be done."

Sarah and Madeline got to work. Inside the goat stall, Sarah got to work raking old hay while Madeline scrubbed the water trough. A rambunctious goat, Clyde, went running and knocked Sarah off her feet and into the water trough, soaking her clothes.

"Aw, man! Clyde, you stinker," said Sarah, with Madeline laughing. Sarah then stood up, slipped, and landed in the mud. She was glad Theo wasn't here to see her.

After they finished taking care of the animals, they went inside Theo's house, Madeline ready to make some lunch. "How do chicken salad sandwiches sound, Sarah?"

"Sounds delicious," replied Sarah. "I sure wish I wasn't all dirty and wet."

"Why don't you go shower and change into some of Theo's clothes? That way, you're comfortable."

"Are you sure? I would feel kind of weird going through his things while he's not home."

"It'll be fine, don't worry about it. You are his girlfriend, after all. Besides, I'm his sister, and I'm giving you permission."

Sarah walked into the large bedroom of the house. It was a deep green color with gorgeous teak wood furniture, a large king-size bed, and another bookshelf. This one had commendations and awards on it from work. Sarah felt very proud of Theo. To the left of the bedroom was a large bathroom with granite countertops, a large bathtub, and a walk-in shower. Inside the bathroom, there was also a walk-in closet. Sarah walked in, still feeling uncomfortable going through Theo's things, so she texted him. "Hey, so I got soaking wet and muddy while cleaning out the stalls, so I'm going to shower at your place and borrow some of your clothes if that's alright."

Theo responded: *lol oh no, yeah, of course that's not a problem.*

Sarah then slipped off her wet and muddy clothes and left them in a pile on the floor. She reached into the shower and turned the handle to hot. Soon, steam started to fill the bathroom. Sarah stepped in, letting the hot water run down her body.

This is nice, thought Sarah.

Sarah then shampooed her hair, but there was no conditioner to be found. She then washed her body and rinsed off. Sarah stepped out of the shower and grabbed a towel, wrapping her hair up in it. She then grabbed another towel and wrapped herself up in it. The towels smelled like Theo. Sarah then went into the closet, looking for a pair of clothes that might fit her. She grabbed a pair of gray sweatpants that had a drawstring. She then grabbed a T-shirt out of the drawer and got dressed. Finally, she combed her hair and dried it with the blow dryer. Feeling refreshed, she walked out to the kitchen where Madeline had just finished preparing lunch.

"Well, you look much better," said Madeline.

"I feel much better. That looks delicious, by the way."

Sarah grabbed a sandwich and started to eat. "So, I had some of your grandma's soup, the magical elixir cold and flu soup. Theo brought some to me when I was sick with a cold."

"Isn't it delicious? It really is magical."

"I'm guessing Theo and his grandma were close?" Sarah just now realized she didn't know much about Theo's whole family, only Madeline and that grandma made good soup.

To be fair, Theo didn't know much about Sarah's family either. "Yes, they were quite close, especially after what happened."

"Um, what did happen?" Sarah was intrigued and also worried about what the answer might be; she didn't want whatever happened to be a horrible incident.

"Oh, Theo didn't tell you then, huh? Well, he doesn't like to talk about it, so I'm not surprised. Well, you see, when Theo was fifteen, and I was nine, we were going somewhere with our parents when we got into a horrible accident. The car was mangled, we were trapped, Theo had broken his leg and wasn't doing well, neither were I and our parents, well, they didn't make it. The paramedics on scene saved Theo's and my life, and that's why Theo became a paramedic after that incident. He wanted to help people the way he was helped and saved. Since our parents didn't make it, we ended up living with our grandma. She and Theo were very close. Theo was always helping her in the kitchen."

Sarah's mouth was agape. She had no idea that was what Theo had been through.

"Oh my gosh, Madeline, I'm so sorry. I had no idea."

"It's okay. I was affected by it a lot when I was younger and went through a crazy rebellious teen phase, bless my poor grandma. But Theo was always there for me.

That, and therapy, ha-ha, but seriously, I don't know what I would have done if I didn't have Theo."

Sarah felt a renewed sense of wonder and awe for Theo. Sarah almost might've said she even loved Theo…almost.

"What about you, Sarah? What about your family?"

"Well, I'm an only child, and my parents sort of had an ugly divorce when I was twelve. I'm pretty close with my mom, and I see my dad occasionally. I thought that was pretty traumatic for me growing up, but nothing compared to you."

"No, your trauma is still valid. That was big for you and changed your world too."

Wow, Madeline must've been a great teacher, validating her student's feelings. All those years of therapy really helped her out. Sarah enjoyed hanging out with Madeline. She almost considered her a friend.

"So Sarah, some friends and I are going to hang out at the Rootin' Tootin' bar if you want to come?"

"I'd love to." Sarah felt touched that Madeline had invited her to hang out. Sarah really liked Madeline.

Hey, Sarah darling, how are things? texted Theo.

They're great. I'm actually hanging out with your sister and her friends at the Rootin' Tootin' bar.

Oh, that's nice. I'm glad you both are getting along so well. I hope she hasn't said anything bad about me or spilled any of my secrets.

Sarah's heart hurt for Theo because of what he went through. Sarah wasn't going to tell him over text, though, that Madeline told her their tragic story.

Nope, nothing bad, yet >:)

I can't wait to see you. Maybe I can come over tomorrow?

Sure thing, after work we can make dinner.

Sarah then remembered the position in NYC and felt a twinge of pain. She enjoyed Madeline's company, and she cared for Theo a whole lot. How could she leave? But again, it was her dream.

"Madeline, if you had a dream job but it required you to move, and you had something worth staying behind for, what would you do?" Sarah asked.

"Well, that's oddly specific. Is this a situation that you're in?"

"Um, no, no, it's just a thought that popped into my head. I figured it was a good conversation starter."

"Well, if it was my dream job, I don't think I could give that up. I would have to find a way to make the thing worth staying for, either come with me, or work it out somehow, or even give it up if it meant I got to follow my dream."

That's what I was afraid of, thought Sarah.

The following day, Sarah woke up with excitement. She was going to see Theo after work. Sarah got up, got dressed, brushed her teeth, and went out into the kitchen, where Rosco was waiting for her. Sarah fed Rosco and then decided what she was going to feed herself. Sarah decided on some eggs and an English muffin. Sarah turned the TV on while she ate. On the news station, they were doing a story about a paramedic who had helped deliver a baby in the woman's car. It was a feel-good story, and it was about Theo. Theo was also receiving an award. Sarah felt so proud of Theo, but why hadn't he told her about it? Sarah would ask him later tonight.

Sarah finished up her breakfast and headed out the door. On her walk to work, she decided to stop by the coffee shop. Sarah opened the door, greeted by the familiar chime of the bell. She was met by the scent of coffee roasting; Two Beans roasted their own coffee beans in-house. Rich woods and pastel yellow walls decorated with folk art welcomed her in. It was quiet inside today, not the usual hustle and bustle of patrons grabbing their morning cup o' joe and a bite to eat. It was peaceful, and Sarah wouldn't have minded staying inside and hanging out if she didn't have to go to work.

"One hazelnut latte to go, please," said Sarah.

"Coming right up. That'll be four-fifty," said the barista. Sarah should've gotten a pastry, they looked delicious, but she was full from breakfast. Sarah grabbed her drink and left.

Sarah got to work and met Jade, who had advised her that the computer had gone down, so there wasn't a way to look at today's dance schedule. Luckily, Sarah was prepared for such situations and had a handwritten schedule. On today's agenda were Ballet I, II, and III, followed by a private lesson. Sarah was focused on work, but in the back of her mind was Theo and seeing him after work. The workday came and went, and Sarah closed up for the day. "So, do you have any fun plans now?" asked coworker Jade.

"Yes, actually, my boyfriend is coming over, and we're going to make dinner." Sarah said, spraying down the computer desk with cleaner.

"That's cute," Jade replied, grabbing some rags to clean up with. Sarah finished up by tidying the counter space.

"Jade do you mind finishing this up and locking up for the night?" said Sarah.

"Sure thing" replied Jade.

"Well, see you later," Sarah said.

"Bye!" replied Jade.

Sarah got home and jumped in the shower. Afterward, she got into some comfy clothes, which reminded her she had to give Theo back the clothes she borrowed. *Knock, knock.*

"That must be Theo," Sarah told Rosco. Sarah walked over to the door and let him in.

"Hey babe," said Theo, and leaned in for a kiss.

"Hey, come on in," said Sarah.

"So what are we having for dinner tonight?" asked Theo.

"I figured we could make spaghetti."

"Sounds delicious."

Sarah and Theo walked into the kitchen. Sarah grabbed a large pot and filled it with water, placing it on the stove and setting the temperature. Theo then grabbed the pasta from the pantry. "I hope you don't mind, but we're making jarred spaghetti sauce," said Sarah. "I don't have the ingredients to make fresh meat sauce."

"A travesty, really," said Theo joking. Soon the water in the pot began to boil, and Sarah placed the spaghetti in the water, splashing her hand with the hot boiling water.

"Ow! Shoot, I got hot water on my hand," Sarah said, drying it off with a towel.

"Oh no, here, let me take a look at it." Theo grabbed Sarah's hand and began examining it, turning on the faucet to cool water. "Here, place your hand under the water and leave it there. The cool water will help," said Theo.

"I think everyone knows to run a burn under cool water," said Sarah sarcastically, sticking her hand under the water. The cool water felt nice against her skin.

Soon, dinner was done cooking, and Theo plated it up. Sarah and Theo sat down on the sofa and began to eat. "So, Theo, the other day when I was at your place in your bedroom, I saw your awards and commendations. I had no idea you received those. I am so proud of you. Why didn't you say anything about them?"

"Oh, I—well, to tell you the truth, I don't like to talk about myself much, and my job is just my job, as in, it's what I do, I would do the same regardless of awards and commendations, so I don't make a big deal out of them."

"Is that why you didn't mention your parents or why you became a paramedic?"

"Madeline told you the story then, huh?" Sarah could feel Theo tense up.

"You could have told me," Sarah said, placing her hand on Theo's leg.

"I know. I just didn't want to depress you or have you worry about me. I'm fine, really. But yes, I became a paramedic because of the ones who saved Mads and me when we were younger after the car accident. The firefighters and police officers who responded were a tremendous help too and also contributed to our life-saving, but I was interested in the medical aspect of saving people."

"Well, I'm sorry you had to go through that. That's awful. I'm glad you were able to follow your dream, though, and become a paramedic. The town of Grenvale is lucky to have you."

"What about you? Is the Grenvale Conservatory your dream job?"

"Did Madeline tell you about the question I asked the other day?"

"Uh, no, why? What did you ask?"

"Oh well, I asked her, 'If you had a dream job, but it required you to move, and you had something worth staying behind for, what would you do?'"

"So, do you have a dream job elsewhere, then?"

"Umm, no, no, nothing like that. It was just a conversational thought that popped into my head. Nothing to worry about."

Sarah didn't like lying to Theo, but she couldn't tell him the truth, not yet anyway.

"And what about your family? Now that you know about my tragic story. I haven't heard you talk about your parents or any siblings," said Theo.

"Well, I'm an only child, and my parents had an ugly divorce when I was twelve. I'm still close to my mom, we talk pretty often, and I see my dad occasionally. That's pretty much all there is to it."

"Oh well, I'm sorry to hear that about your parents."

Speaking of Sarah's mom, Sarah hadn't told her yet of Theo. She would have to do that and maybe explain the situation she is in. Sarah's mom was always good at navigating difficult situations.

The night carried on, with Theo and Sarah conversing and snuggling on the sofa. "So Sarah, there's something I wanted to ask you. My sister Madeline is getting married, and I wanted to ask if you would be my date for the wedding." Wedding dates were a big deal.

"Oh, I love weddings. Of course, I'll be your date to Madeline's wedding," said Sarah.

Soon after, it was time for Theo to leave. "I have to get going, but I had a real fun time. The spaghetti was delicious, even with your jarred sauce. Next time I'll have to make my grandmother's sauce," said Theo fondly.

"Sounds good, can't wait to try it. Talk later?"

"You bet, goodbye darling," and with a kiss, Theo was out the door. There was that twinge of pain in Sarah's chest again; lying to Theo didn't help.

Chapter 14

"Hi, Mom. How are you?" Sarah said into the phone.

"I'm good, sweety, how are you? How's the dance school?"

"I've been good, and the Conservatory has been really good. Oh, I do have some good news, though. I have a boyfriend now."

"Oh yeah? Well, what's his name? What's he like?"

"His name is Theo," Sarah said, going on to describe him and what he does. "He's very well-read, intelligent, handsome, and he's a paramedic in town, but Mom, I'm in a pickle and don't know what to do. I need your advice. There is a position available that is my dream job, but it would require me to move away and leave Grenvale behind, thus leaving Theo behind. Theo has his stuff here in Grenvale, so I wouldn't ask him to come along with me. Besides, we haven't even been together that long anyway. We haven't even said the L word yet. I just don't know what to do."

"Oh, sweety, that's a tough one. It's really hard to say what the right decision is. You have to be the one to decide what is best for you. I guess you can start by determining if the dream job is actually your dream job and go from there. Sorry, I can't be more of any help, honey."

"Gee, thanks, Mom." Sarah then had an idea, what if she went to NYC and trialed the job for a little while, just to see if it was something she truly wanted to do. "Mom, I have to go. I've got to make a phone call. Talk to you later."

"Bye, sweety." Sarah brought out her computer and pulled up the job listing. Sarah was going to apply for the position but asked if she could try it first. Sarah hit the apply button and filled out the form, then with a deep breath, she hit submit. Immediately after, she called the New York City School of American Ballet.

"Hi, my name is Sarah Shuster, and I just applied for the position of teacher. I was wondering, though, if it was at all possible to come try the position beforehand. I would come work at the school for a period of time, and then at the end of that time, we would decide if I'm a good fit and see if I stay on permanently."

The school, to Sarah's surprise, was on board with the idea of trialing the position. It would work out for them cause they would have someone fill the spot, at least temporarily, and would possibly gain a full-time permanent teacher out of it. The school didn't have much to lose.

"Yes, ma'am, we'll go ahead and send you confirmation in the mail."

Sarah was excited, but she still hadn't told Theo. A few days later, a piece of mail came for Sarah. It was from the New York City School of American Ballet.

Dear Ms. Shuster,

It is with great honor that we welcome you aboard our team of highly educated and skilled members. Should you accept, we will begin trialing you come June fifth. You will work for two months, at which time you can decide if you would like to stay a permanent member of the team. We look forward to hearing from you soon.

Signed,

Laura Doone

Executive Director

Sarah squealed with delight and danced around her condo. She can't believe she got the position. She had landed her dream job. And this way, she still had some time to think about if this was what she really wanted and what she was going to do about Theo. Sarah wished she could just text Theo the good news right away, but she better tell him to his face.

A few days later, Theo was over again. Sarah had gone to the bathroom when Theo accidentally knocked the letter off the counter onto the floor. Theo picked it up and read it. *What? She's leaving for NYC? Why didn't she tell me?* Theo thought. Theo then placed the letter back on the counter.

Sarah came back out of the bathroom and realized she left the letter on the counter. *Theo wouldn't go reading my stuff without my permission, would he?* Sarah thought. *No, it's fine.*

Sarah, however, noticed Theo was acting distant but wasn't sure why.

"Theo, is everything okay? You seem a little distant today." Sarah said rubbing Theo's back.

"Yes, I'm fine, sorry, I was just thinking about work, is all." Theo said, placing his hand on Sarah's.

"Okay, if you're sure. Do you want to talk about it?"

"No, I'll be okay," said Theo.

Sarah thought, *Okay, now is a good time to tell him. Just let him know that you got your dream position and you'll be gone for only two months. Easy Peasy.*

Sarah then said, "Theo, there's something I have to tell you."

"Sure, what is it? You can tell me anything," Theo said, wondering if it was about the letter.

"Well, I—" Sarah paused. Theo placed his hand on her thigh and looked her in the eyes. He could see she was searching for what to say. "What I wanted to say was that…I…like you a lot. Like so much. I enjoy spending time with you. Your company is my favorite," Sarah said, unable to bring up the job due to nerves and being afraid about what might happen if she did.

"Oh, well, I like you a lot too, Sarah. You mean so much to me," Theo responded with a smile on his face.

Just tell him, thought Sarah to herself.

Why won't she tell me about New York? Theo thought. Sarah and Theo finished hanging out, when Theo said "it's getting late, I better get going" and left for the night, still wondering why Sarah wouldn't bring up the NYC letter.

*****

"Ugh, come on, Sarah, why didn't you say anything? He was right there, and you had the letter," said Jessie the next day.

"I don't know, I just chickened out and panicked, I suppose."

"By the way, I'm still mad you didn't tell me about it right away. So I know how Theo will feel," Jessie said. "Anyway, I'm so proud of you. Congratulations."

"Thanks. I think."

"So you're going to take the job and be gone for two months? What about the Conservatory here?"

"Jade will take over for me while I'm gone. And if I decide to stay permanently, she'll take over and hire a new teacher."

"Have you told them about the position yet at the Conservatory?"

"Well, Jade was the one who told me they were hiring in the first place. I think they expected me to apply."

"And, of course, you would get the position. You're crazy talented and a great teacher."

Sarah grinned. "I'm nervous, though," Sarah said.

"That's understandable. It's a new venture. It can be a little scary. When are you going to tell Theo?" Jessie said.

"I'm not sure. I don't know how to tell him," responded Sarah.

Chapter 15

Theo was at work at the fire station and told Trevor about Sarah's note. "Yeah, man, I don't know, Sarah hasn't said anything to me, but I know what I saw in that letter. She got a position at the New York City School of American Ballet, which I mean is amazing for her, but why wouldn't she tell me?" asked Theo.

"Maybe she doesn't know how to tell you. I mean, this position would mean that she would be leaving Grenvale, and you're here. She might not know what to do," Trevor responded.

"I'm sure we can think of something, even if it's being in a long-distance relationship, or I could move with her, maybe."

"And give up your homestead? That's probably why Sarah hasn't asked you or told you. She doesn't want you to give up what you have," Trevor said.

"Well, I would leave the homestead to Madeline, probably. I'm sure she would take care of it, and there's you, too. You could continue assisting her like you've been doing," Theo said.

"Well, I don't know what to tell you, man. Maybe you should just talk to her."

Trevor was right. Theo should have just talked to Sarah.

Theo texted Sarah: *Hey beautiful, I miss you. I'd like to see you again. Maybe you can come over to my place tomorrow? Just let me know.*

Ding. Theo's phone went off: *Hey you, that sounds like a plan, be there at 5:00?*

Sounds good, replied Theo. Just then, the alarm sounded, which meant Theo and Trevor had a call to respond to. They geared up and jumped in the ambulance.

The call: a horrific car accident with entrapment. Theo felt his pulse quicken, and his breath got shallow. In his years of working as a paramedic, he has responded to other vehicle crashes, but none as severe as this one. Theo flashed back to his own tragic accident when he was a teenager, trapped in the vehicle with a broken leg screaming for help.

"Get it together, Theo. This is what you train for. Focus on your job. You can deal with the emotions later." Theo thought to himself.

Trevor must have picked up on Theo's unease, asking him if he was okay.

"Theo, buddy, you going to be okay?"

"Yes. I'll get through it."

But Theo wasn't sure if he would be okay. In that moment, all he wanted was Sarah's arms wrapped around him, her soft velvety lips pressed against his.

"C'mon Theo, get your head in the game. Focus. Relax. Breathe. Focus. Relax. Breathe," Theo kept telling himself.

Once on scene, Theo's training kicked into gear, and he performed his tasks and duties flawlessly. At the scene was a mangled vehicle overturned, and trapped inside were two small children, a boy and a girl. The two adults in the vehicle were in critical condition. Firefighters used the jaws of life to rescue the family. Due to the nature of the call, there were two ambulances on the scene, one for the parents and one for the children. Theo took over the children's care.

"Hey, sweety," Theo said to the young girl. "I'm right here with you. I'm not leaving you." They were being transported to the hospital. It was not clear if the two adults were going to make it. Theo was definitely going to need a debriefing after this call. Theo got back to the station and started the debrief with a peer support specialist. Theo didn't want to talk about anything, though, cause Theo didn't like to talk about himself or his problems.

The next day, Theo couldn't wait for Sarah to come over. Theo had spent all morning cleaning up the house, making it look spotless for Sarah. Sarah arrived at 5:00 on the dot. Theo planned on cooking out on the grill. The weather was nice, so he figured they could sit outside and have dinner by the fire pit. For dinner, he had planned barbecue chicken with roasted corn on the cob and asparagus, and mashed potatoes. For dessert, Sarah's favorite, s'mores.

Theo heard Sarah's car pull up and went out to greet her. "Hi, sweety," Theo said.

"Hey babe," Sarah responded. "How was your drive over?"

"It was fine, not bad at all. There was no traffic, so that helped a lot."

"Good, good, glad to hear it." Was it just Sarah, or was Theo acting sort of off?

They walked inside, and Sarah immediately walked over to the bookshelf. Sarah wanted to look at Theo's bookshelf some more and see what other books he had on it. He had some more classics on it, like *Animal Farm* by George Orwell, *Anthem* by Ayn Rand, *The Call of the Wild* by Jack London, and of course, *Sense and Sensibility* by Jane Austen. Sarah was impressed and jealous at the collection of books he had. His bookshelf was huge, spanning the entire wall, floor to ceiling; it even had one of those rolling ladders attached to it. Sarah remembered that Theo wrote and wondered if he would share some of his writings with her. Dinner was ready, and Theo and Sarah headed outside.

While eating, Sarah brought up Theo's writing. "Babe, I know you said that you were a writer, that you wrote poetry and some novels. Do you think I could read your writings? I'm very interested."

"Oh, well, I don't think they're that great, but sure, for you, I'll let you read them," and Theo disappeared inside the house. He came out with a stack of papers and handed them to Sarah. Sarah took the first one that Theo said was from his younger days and read it:

A calm lake

smooth as glass,

receives kisses from the moonlight.

This is where peace sleeps.

At least for now,

until the day comes

and sheds light on the town.

The statuesque trees, larger than life,

stand at attention

right out of sight.

There is a deafening silence.

At least for now.

Sarah was taken by the beauty of the poetry she just read. This man that was hers wrote that. Sarah felt unbelievably lucky. She grabbed another poem and read it:

Her lips pursed, a ruby red

Her skin soft, alabaster white

Her hair, a fawn on her head

Her touch electrifying.

She made his heart quiver and tremble at first sight.

She was beauty.

She was perfection.

And yet, she never saw him.

Her eyes looked his way,

but he disappeared among the crowd,

just another figure.

And thus, he was left with a broken heart.
The woman he could never have.

"Theo, these are really good. Have you ever thought about being published?"

"Oh no, I hadn't given that much thought. I don't know if I want my stuff out there."

"Well, you should totally think about it," said Sarah.

And then, "Hey, Theo, are you okay? You seem a little off today. I want to make sure you're alright."

Theo pulled Sarah in close for a hug, Sarah melting into his strong muscular arms, smelling his cologne. "I'm fine, baby. I just had a tough call at work yesterday. I did a debrief after, and it helped some, although I didn't talk much."

"Oh, do you want to talk about it? What kind of call was it? And what exactly is a debrief?"

"It was a bad car accident with entrapment. I sort of had a flashback to my own accident. A debrief is when you get with your peers and a peer support specialist and talk about what happened. You talk about the call, what you did, how you responded, what you think went right and what you think went wrong, what could have been done better, etc."

"Oh no, Theo, I'm so sorry you had to deal with that. Well, I'm here for you no matter what."

Theo didn't want to ruin this perfect moment, and he wasn't really angry, but he wanted to ask, "Will you, though? Will you always be here for me no matter what, even if you're in New York?" But Theo was enjoying Sarah's company, and he was sure she would come around and tell him soon.

*****

Finally, it was time for Madeline's wedding. Sarah wore a plum-colored gown that made her eyes pop. This was a good opportunity for her to forget all about her decision-making and not telling Theo and just enjoy love and have fun. Theo was in the wedding party, and so he was already at the venue when Sarah showed up. Seeing Sarah made Theo's heart skip a beat.

"Sarah, wow, you look stunning," said Theo.

"Oh, this old thing?" teased Sarah. "How's Madeline doing?"

"She's good. She's pretty much ready. Do you want to see her?" asked Theo, gently placing his hand on Sarah's back.

"Sure," replied Sarah. Theo then took Sarah's hand and led her to a getting-ready room where Madeline was waiting. The getting-ready room was a smaller room that had a vanity with a mirror on it, a full-length mirror at the opposite side of the room, and a small sofa in between the two, set against the wall.

"Oh, Madeline, you look absolutely stunning," Sarah said, walking over to hug Madeline, who was sitting at the vanity.

"Oh, thank you, you look very nice yourself."

"Well, I don't want to keep you, I'm sure you still have a lot of getting ready to do, so I'm going to head to my seat."

"Do you want me to walk you to your seat?" asked Theo.

"No, I'll be okay. I can find my way. A lot of the seats are already taken, though. I feel like everyone is going to stare at me."

"Only because of how gorgeous you are," Theo said, causing Sarah to blush.

Sarah walked out and went to her seat. Soon the processional music started, and the bridal party walked down the aisle. Then 'Canon in D' started playing, and everyone stood up.

Soon Madeline appeared, looking radiant with a big smile across her face. Up the aisle was the groom, Jared, who had a few tears running down his face at the sight of his beautiful bride. The wedding ceremony itself was quite short but lovely. Then came time for the reception, or big party after the ceremony. Sarah was looking for Theo, who was busy mingling with other people that were in attendance. Theo finally got a moment free and sought out Sarah. They made eye contact across the floor and made their way over to each other.

"That was a beautiful ceremony," said Sarah.

"Yes, it was quite lovely," Theo said, his eyes misty. His baby sister was now a married woman; that would take some getting used to. "Shall I have this dance?" Theo asked. Theo then grabbed Sarah's waist and hand and started twirling around. Soon, the whole room melted away for Sarah, and she was only present with Theo.

Theo grabbed Sarah's chin and lifted her face toward him when, "Ahem," said the coordinator, causing Sarah to snap back to where she was. "Theo, it's time for speeches," said the coordinator.

Sarah felt a little embarrassed but also disappointed. She wanted that kiss from Theo. Theo gave his speech and then returned to Sarah, who had developed a headache.

"Theo, I think I'm going to go. I'm not feeling well."

"Okay, do you need me to take you home?"

"No, I'll be able to make it."

"Okay, lo—I'll talk to you later. Make it home safely."

Did Theo almost say he loved Sarah?

A couple days had passed since the wedding, and Sarah and Theo continued to hang out, this one time going on the picnic they wanted the last time they went hiking. Sarah still not telling Theo about the New York job. On their hike/picnic, Sarah packed up some peanut butter and jelly sandwiches and snacks. It was a fun time, despite Theo being concerned about Sarah not telling him about New York.

Then one day, Sarah was hanging out at Theo's house. She was there helping with the animals, feeding them and cleaning out the stalls, tending to the garden, watering the plants, and planting new crops. Theo asked Sarah how she had been, how work was going, thinking it would be a good way to lead Sarah into telling Theo about the job, but she still wouldn't say anything. It wasn't that Sarah didn't want to. Of course, she wanted to tell him, but telling him would make it real.

Telling him would mean they would have to figure out what to do about them. Sarah couldn't ask Theo to give up what he had and come with her, but she didn't want to lose Theo either. There was always the option of a long-distance relationship, but how would that work? Would Theo even be willing to try that? There were too many questions for Sarah, and that's why she wouldn't tell him, not yet.

Theo was starting to lose patience with Sarah for not telling him. Why was she keeping it a big secret? Theo thought about coming clean to her about seeing the letter, but he didn't want confrontation. Theo decided to ask Sarah to dinner and would ask her about it finally then. At 6:00 PM, Theo picked up Sarah for their dinner date. It started out as any other dinner date, and Sarah was excited. They were headed to their favorite place, Mama Melrose's. Sarah had been wanting her usual pizza.

"Hi, Haddie!" said Sarah walking into the restaurant. "You remember Theo?"

"Oh yes, how could I forget. Hi Theo. What can I get for y'all today?"

Theo ordered the spicy pepperoni calzone, the same one Jessie usually orders. Sarah ordered her usual pepperoni, green pepper, and mushroom pizza and a Coke.

Sarah and Theo had a pleasant conversation and enjoyed their dinner. Finally, Theo gathered up the courage to confront Sarah about the New York job.

"Sarah, remember when the other day, you said you would always be here for me?"

"Yes, of course, 'cause it's true."

Here goes, Theo thought. "Okay, well, how about when you're in New York, hmm? How will you be here for me if you're there?"

Sarah stared at Theo, mouth agape. "Theo, I don't—" Sarah stammered, tears stinging her eyes. "How do you know about that?" asked Sarah tearfully.

"I accidentally knocked your letter off your counter. When I picked it up, I saw what it said. So you're leaving to go to New York, and you didn't tell me."

"Theo, I wanted to tell you, I hated keeping it a secret from you, but I didn't know how to tell you. There were too many unanswered questions, and I was afraid of what the answers might be if I brought them up."

"Sarah, I care about you so much. We could've worked it all out together. You should have had more faith and trust in me. I think you or I should go now."

"Theo, please—"

"I just need some time. I had a stressful day at work yesterday and then this. Just please give me some space."

Sarah got up with tears streaming down her cheeks. She never meant for this to happen. How could she hurt the person she cared about most? Sarah got into her car and left. Arriving home, she was greeted by Rosco, who could tell she was sad.

"Hi, Rosco," Sarah said, still crying. "I really messed up big time. I wonder if Jessie is up, I could use a listening ear right about now." Sarah called Jessie, but it went to voicemail. Sarah, still crying, left an urgent voicemail for Jessie to call her back. Sarah then went and got ready for bed, crawled into bed, curled up into a ball, and fell asleep to her tears streaming down her face.

The next morning, Sarah had an urgent voicemail back from Jessie, asking Sarah what was wrong and what the urgency was for. Sarah called Jessie.

"Hello? Sarah?"

"Hi Jessie," Sarah's voice hoarse from crying, her eyes red and puffy.

"Sarah, oh my gosh, what's wrong? Are you okay?"

"No, I think Theo broke up with me, or maybe he didn't, but he seemed upset, and I don't know what to do."

"Well, what happened?"

"He confronted me about New York. He said he saw the letter and that I didn't tell him about it."

"Well, you sort of didn't tell him about it, so he's not wrong."

"I know, I know, he has every right to be upset. It's just that I meant to tell him. I didn't like keeping it from him. I didn't know how to tell him."

"Well, I'm sure you can fix the situation. Just give him some time and space like he asked."

Chapter 16

Days went by without much contact between Theo and Sarah. Sarah had tried texting and calling Theo, but Theo always answered with short, curt replies or didn't pick up the phone. They hadn't seen each other since the day of the fight. In the beginning, Sarah had been so worried about getting burned and getting her heart broken again that she never once thought she would be the one to break someone's heart.

At work, everyone was excited for Sarah and her new endeavor. Jade was getting ready to take over as lead teacher and was learning all the ropes and administrative things that needed to be done. The students were going to miss Ms. Shuster, but most of them were so talented Sarah wouldn't be surprised if her students ended up at the New York City School of American Ballet.

June 5th was fast approaching, and Sarah had to get ready and pack for her new adventure. She packed up all her clothes, or as many clothes as she could fit into the two large suitcases she was bringing, as well as other items she might need. Sarah got the necessary paperwork ready for the job, such as the letter and her identification, paperwork for the place she was going to be staying at, and paperwork for Rosco, like his shots list, as Rosco was obviously coming with Sarah to NYC. Jessie was over, helping Sarah pack up so they could spend some time together before Sarah had to leave.

"Man, I'm really going to miss you and us hanging out, especially at Rootin' Tootin'," said Jessie.

"I know. I'm going to miss you and our girls' nights. You'll have to definitely come to visit me while I'm up in New York," said Sarah. Sarah was getting ready to leave and still felt so sad that Theo was practically ignoring her. All she wanted was for him to forgive her with a hug and a kiss.

*****

Meanwhile, on Theo's homestead, Theo had been sulking around, and both Madeline and Trevor picked up on his change of mood and behavior. "C'mon Theo, I'm sure she's sorry for lying to you, or at least not telling you the truth. You said yourself she wanted to tell you she just didn't know how," said Madeline.

"Yeah, but how can she not know how? You just say, 'Hey Theo, I got my dream position in New York City.'"

"Well, you have to think about it from her position. She obviously likes and cares about you a lot, and you're here in Grenvale, and she's going to be twenty-five hundred miles away from you. It must've been such a hard decision for her to have to make," Trevor said.

"You're right. Maybe I'll go talk to her. I work tomorrow, so I hope she doesn't leave so soon, so I can actually see her."

The following day Sarah was supposed to leave for New York. However, they delayed her flight by one day. Would Theo be able to make it in time to see her before she left? Theo texted Sarah: *Hey, I'm sorry I've been distant. I just needed some space. I'd really like to see you. I hope tomorrow is okay.*

Hey, that's fine. I'd like to see you too. My plane leaves at 3:00, so I have to be at the airport at 1:00, so you have until then.

The next day, Theo woke up late cause his alarm didn't go off, it was 11:00, and Theo only had about an hour and a half to go see Sarah. Theo got up quickly, brushed his teeth and got dressed, and ran out of the house to his truck. Theo climbed into the truck, put the key in the ignition, turned the key, and *click click click*, his car wouldn't start. Theo tried turning the key again: *click click click*, still wouldn't turn on.

"You have got to be kidding me!" cried Theo. Theo quickly called Madeline, "Hey, Mads, I was on my way to go see Sarah, but my truck is dead. I need a jump or to borrow your car." Why didn't Theo have a portable jump pack? He had been meaning to purchase one, he just never got around to it.

"Hey, sorry, I don't get out of school until 3:40. I don't think you can wait till then. Try Trevor. Maybe he might be able to assist you," said Madeline.

Theo then called Trevor. "Hey, bud, are you still in town? I was on my way to go see Sarah, but my truck is dead. I need a jump or to borrow your car or get a ride."

"Naw man, sorry we already left town, can't help you there," replied Trevor. It seemed Theo was out of luck. Theo called a mechanic who said they could be there within thirty minutes. Theo only had an hour before Sarah left. The mechanic took longer with his last job and got to Theo late, and spent some time working on the car as it was more than just the battery being dead. That was the problem with the truck. Theo thanked the mechanic, then jumped in the truck and sped off toward Sarah's house. He hoped he wasn't too late.

Theo raced over to Sarah's house, ready to profess his love for her. When Theo arrived, he threw his truck in park and flew up the stairs to Sarah's condo and knocked on the door. There was no answer. Theo was too late. Sarah had already left for the airport. Theo whipped out his phone and tried dialing Sarah's number, it went straight to voicemail. Theo then wrote out a text message and tried sending it, but it wouldn't go through. Theo had no way of getting in contact with Sarah now.

*****

Sarah had everything packed up and was finishing the final touches of getting together whatever she needed for her flight to NYC. Sarah paced nervously, waiting for Theo to show up, but he never did. Jessie showed up at 12:30, ready to take Sarah to the airport.

"So Theo never showed up?" asked Jessie.

"No, he never showed up," said Sarah sadly, with a tear running down her cheek. She was going away from Grenvale for at least two months and didn't even get to say goodbye to her boyfriend. Sarah and Jessie left Sarah's condo and left for the airport.

*****

Sarah had made the move and arrived in New York City. She was excited to start her job at the ballet school. She also really liked her little one-bedroom, one-bathroom apartment that she got, even if it was four flights of stairs up with no elevator. That meant she and Rosco got their exercise. Sarah's apartment was small and cozy, with a lot of beige and neutral colors filling the space. Sarah also had some plants inside to bring some color and life to the place. In her living room, she didn't have a fireplace like in her condo, so she hung up a set of fairy curtain lights up instead.

To the right of the living room was a small kitchen. Real small, as in only having one cabinet down below and one cabinet up above, with a fridge that wasn't a mini fridge, but it wasn't full size either. There was just enough counter space for a cutting board and coffee pot and a sink. Sarah liked the location. It was close to a bodega where she would get her chopped cheese and a coffee. There was also a coffee shop around the corner, it wasn't Two Beans, but it was nice.

It was Sarah's first day of her job. She woke up at her usual 5:00 AM and did her exercise routine. She did thirty minutes on the treadmill, which fit between her couch and TV, and then did some weighted exercises. After, she jumped in the shower and brushed her teeth. Sarah then went to the kitchen to feed Rosco and herself. She decided on some oatmeal with fresh berries today and packed herself a yogurt with granola for a snack later. Sarah also packed her lunch. She made herself a turkey wrap and brought some baby carrots with ranch dressing. Sarah then finished getting ready and headed out the door.

The Conservatory was not too far from Sarah's apartment but did require her to take the subway. Lucky for Sarah, she lived only a ten-minute walk to the subway platform. The Conservatory was located on 65th Street between Amsterdam and Broadway, at the corner of the Lincoln Center Campus. Sarah took the #1 local train to the 66th Street station. She then only had to walk one block south to West 65th Street.

Across the street on Broadway was a movie theater and some stores. A few blocks down the street was a coffee shop. Sarah was excited for work but felt the familiar gnawing pain in her chest. She couldn't completely get her mind off of Theo, and she couldn't get their last conversation out of her head. She missed him and wondered if he missed her.

Sarah walked into work for her first day and was greeted by Laura Doone, the one who signed the acceptance letter. Mrs. Doone was the executive director at the school. She welcomed Sarah in and gave her a tour of the campus. Sarah was impressed with what she saw. There were dozens of talented students practicing in gorgeous classrooms that were spacious and full of light. Sarah then met some of the other instructors that she would be working alongside. Sarah felt like she fit right in.

*****

Meanwhile, back in Grenvale, Theo had been moping around, sad that he couldn't see Sarah before she left, though not for lack of trying. Though Theo wanted to see Sarah, he was still hurt by her lack of trust in him. That's why he didn't make any effort to call her, he was still upset with what went down, and he wanted to see Sarah face to face to reconcile their problems. Madeline had been over and noticed how pouty Theo was being.

"Theo, you have to do something or get over the situation. You can't keep being pouty and moody like you are."

"Hmph," grunted Theo.

"Why don't you just call her and let her know how you feel?"

"Because I want to see her face to face to do that. Besides, for me to tell her how I feel, that I—well, I—"

"You what, Theo? How do you really feel about Sarah? You should go to her if you care that much. Run to her and fix this, fix you."

Chapter 17

It had been one week since Sarah started her new job. She liked it a lot, but she missed Grenvale, she missed her condo there, she missed Jessie, the Conservatory, her students, and she missed Theo. She was here at the SAB (School of American Ballet) for only three weeks out of her two months trial, and she could see herself continuing to work here past that, but she had to decide if she was willing to give up her life in Grenvale for good. It was a hard decision that Sarah was stressed about making.

Sarah finished up her work day of intensive ballet classes with the very talented students that blew Sarah's mind. Sarah had been thrilled to work with students of such a high caliber. Sarah thought about her students at the Conservatory and how talented they were and thought that they would fit in perfectly here. If only she could bring all of them over to the SAB.

"Okay, class, great job, everyone. We're done for today. Don't forget to go home and practice what we learned today." Most students lived on campus and were free to use the practice rooms whenever they wanted.

Sarah got home and got changed into some comfier clothing; sweatpants and a T-shirt. She was about to sit down with some delicious pad thai that she had delivered and a glass of wine when there was a knock at her door. Sarah, unsure who it could be, walked over to the door and opened it.

"Surprise!" Jessie yelled, startling Sarah.

"Jessie?" Sarah asked, stunned. "Oh my god, Jessie!" Sarah said when she regained her composure. "What are you doing here?" Sarah asked.

"Surprising you, silly! What do you think?"

"Well, consider me surprised. Oh my gosh, come on in." Sarah moved to the side as Jessie walked in.

Sarah's order of pad thai was quite big, so Sarah offered Jessie some of hers. "I had ordered myself some food, but it's way too much for me to eat. I was going to have leftovers, but do you want some instead? You're probably hungry after traveling all this way," Sarah said handing the takeout container over to Jessie.

"Sure, I'd love some." Jessie said grabbing a plate.

"It's just like old times, huh? Our girls' nights we used to have."

"Sure is. I missed those." Jessie said as she took a big bite of the Pad Thai.

"Even though I've only been gone three weeks, ha-ha." Sarah said.

Jessie then got quiet for a moment before asking, "So, have you heard from Theo?"

"No," answered Sarah sadly, taking a bite of her own food.

"He hasn't called you or anything?" asked Jessie.

"No, not a single phone call. I assume he's still mad at me and doesn't want to talk."

"Oh, Sarah, I'm sure he'll forgive you and reach out to you soon, don't give up just yet. Have you tried calling him to see if he'll answer?"

"No, I figured he doesn't want to talk to me, so it would be too painful if I called and he didn't answer." Sarah said curling up onto the sofa.

"Well, come on, girl, break out some more of that wine, and let's forget all about that for now." Sarah got up and grabbed two wine glasses and a bottle of cabernet, then settled back on the sofa.

A few weeks had passed, and Sarah had been enjoying her job and living in NYC. She had been getting around easily and enjoyed exploring everything the city had to offer. She went and saw the empire state building and some performances on Broadway. She also went and visited Rockefeller Center, Radio City Music Hall, and time square. It was a huge city and so offered a much different experience than Grenvale.

One day, Sarah was at work teaching a class when there was a large commotion at the front desk of the SAB with a person heard saying loudly, "But I need to talk to her. I need to see Sarah Shuster."

"Only students are allowed back in the school," said the front desk attendant. Sarah, approaching the commotion and hearing her name, was confused and concerned until she laid eyes on the person.

With surprise in her voice, she said, "Theo?" Theo turned around. Were his eyes deceiving him? Was Sarah even more beautiful than he remembered?

"Sarah," said Theo as Sarah took a step toward Theo. Theo rushed over to Sarah.

"Sir!" yelled the front desk attendant, but Theo didn't listen.

Sarah ran into his arms. "Theo! What are you doing here?" asked Sarah, still in disbelief her boyfriend was here at her job.

"I had to see you. I couldn't take the silence anymore. I needed to hold you and kiss you. You mean so much to me, and I want us to work us out and work this situation out. I know we can do it. And—"

"And what?" said Sarah with tears in her eyes.

"And I love you, Sarah Shuster. I love you more than you could ever know. I want to be with you. I'll give up my homestead and my job if it means I get to be with you. I'll give the homestead to Madeline, and I'll become a paramedic here in NYC, or even better, I'll become a published writer. I just need to be with you."

Sarah had tears streaming down her cheeks. "Oh, Theo. I love you too! I missed you so much, and I miss Grenvale and the Conservatory and my students and Jessie. You know what? This job has been an amazing experience, and I am so glad I had the opportunity to do this. But I'm realizing this job isn't meant for me long term. What do you say we return to Grenvale, and you can return to your homestead and paramedic career, and I'll be right by your side."

Then, Theo stepped right up to Sarah, putting one arm around her waist and the other hand through her hair, tilted her head back, and placed his lips on her lush, velvety pink lips and kissed her with all the passion he had been saving up for her. Sarah was left breathless with shivers down her spine, and her cheeks were the color of fresh salmon, blushing hard at the public display of affection Theo just gave her. Sarah then invited Theo over to her place. Sarah walked up to the front desk attendant and notified her that a few days from now would be her last day working at the SAB, for she was leaving back to Grenvale with Theo.

Epilogue

Four Months Later

Sarah had moved back to Grenvale into her old condo with Rosco and went back to her old teaching position at the Conservatory, which Jade was real happy about to have her coworker and friend back. Theo had gone back to his paramedic job, working once again alongside his buddy Trevor.

One day while on a date, Theo had invited Sarah to move in with him. Sarah had been looking forward to moving out of her condo and into Theo's house with him. She enjoyed how spacious it was, and she enjoyed his book collection. She had also been looking forward to helping on the farm, along with Madeline and Trevor.

Sarah and Theo had many more dates, often visiting Haddie at Mama Melrose's for some delicious pizza and calzones. They also spent their time, when not working on the farm, hiking the trails and playing with Rosco and Zoe, as well as bowling, since Theo needed to work on his game. He still threw gutter balls, while Sarah managed to get some strikes and spares.

One nice end of summer night, everyone was out at Theo's place as Theo had organized a huge cookout. Theo, Trevor, Jessie, Haddie, Jade, Madeline, Jared and Sarah were all there.

Theo was grilling burgers and hot dogs, and the rest of them were gathered around the fire pit and hanging out in the pool. Music was blasting and there was just all-around fun being had. They had all been eating and drinking, enjoying each other's company and the nice weather out, when Theo got everyone's attention.

"Attention, everybody" Theo shouted. There was a buzzing energy in the air.

"Shh, quiet down," someone said.

"Hey guys, thank you all so much for being here tonight. I really appreciate it. Now, it's no secret that I am crazy about Sarah. Sarah, you know how much I love you. You are just amazing and perfect, and I couldn't ask for anyone better. With that said, I know I want to spend the rest of my life with you," Theo said, getting down on one knee and pulling a small blue velvet box out of his pocket. "Sarah Shuster, will you do the honor of being mine forever and marry me?" Theo said opening up the box to display a gorgeous antique-style engagement ring.

"Theo…" said Sarah with a tear running down her face and her hands covering her mouth. "Yes! Of course, I'll marry you." Sarah exclaimed as she jumped up. She grabbed the sides of Theo's face and kissed him. Everyone cheered and celebrated.

"Woohoo!" Shouted someone.

"Congratulations man" Trevor said.

"Let me see that ring" Jessie said, grabbing for Sarah's left hand. After some of the excitement settled down and the group went back to their eating and drinking and playing around, Sarah snuggled into Theo, pressing her head into his chest, and checking out the ring that was on her finger. It was a good night.